IF
ONLY

IF ONLY

JENNIFER GILMORE

HARPER TEEN
An Imprint of HarperCollinsPublishers

HarperTeen is an imprint of HarperCollins Publishers.

If Only

Library of Congress Control Number: 2018933330
ISBN 978-0-06-239363-0

Typography by Jessie Gang
18 19 20 21 22 PC/LSCH 10 9 8 7 6 5 4 3 2 1

First Edition

For Julian

IF
ONLY

PART 1

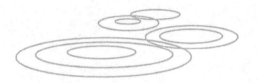

BRIDGET

Will the sweetness swallow all the bitter? Is that a way to start a letter? I knock the pen against the side of my head like I'm taking a cartoon test and I'm cartoon-thinking. What would I say? If I were to write a letter, I mean. My pen—pretty, peach-colored. It says *Be Brave* along the side.

"Really?" I had said to Dahlia when she gave it to me. I'd held it out to her, like I wanted to give it back.

"Really," she'd said. "My mother gave it to me when I started getting into coloring books again."

I'm wondering this—sweet bitter—while I'm waiting for Dahlia now at the café. I have no idea. I mean I'm sixteen, but I am not a total mess. I have done things I'm not proud of, I've made some bad choices, true, but I am not on drugs and I'm not about to start now. My family will help. I can do this, I am thinking, but I am also thinking that I can't. Do this. Not even for her.

I know it's a her.

She is.

"Bridge," Dahlia says. "Hi, honey," she says, shaking off rain.

She takes off her hat. There's that smell of rain, too. I know you know it.

"Thanks for meeting," I say.

This is our winter place now, but we're inching toward spring. We like the table in the nook that hangs over the creek. It's out of the way here, an extra ten-minute walk, but we do it and when we do we know it's serious.

"Of course. What's up? Why so crazy urgent?"

"You want hot chocolate or something? Cider?" Also they have amazing hot chocolate.

"What's up?" Dahlia asks me again. "Your hair looks good by the way." She reaches out and pulls the chunk of pink I dyed last night. My private celebration I think. Because last night I'd decided.

But anything changes my mind. All kinds of thoughts. People. A photo in a magazine. A girl with headphones alone on the street. A woman holding a wobbly toddler's hand.

"I want to keep it," I say.

She looks up. "That's insane. You can't. You and your mom already decided. *We* decided. Are you insane?"

"When I think about it I can't stop crying. I can't."

"Let's look at some more profiles from the agency. You will find the right people. They will be the right parents."

"Will they be, though?"

"My mom's adopted," Dahlia says. "Remember?"

"Gorgeous Lulu! I always forget that part about her."

"Closed. All the paperwork. She's got no idea who her birth parents are. Could be anyone. She looked for a long time. This is so different. The baby will know who you are. She will hear you laughing. My mom always says mine was the first laugh that she recognized."

But what if I never laugh again? My heart, I think, is breaking. Dahlia's mom. I can't help but think of her dad, Raymond, too, all messed up from the Vietnam War like so many of the fathers in this town. Mine, too. They got drafted—no choices at all. Go there. Kill people. Come home. What kind of a choice is that?

Our mothers aren't friends anymore.

Their mothers were best friends, too. Valerie and Lulu. Both their boyfriends went away and came back, changed. That's when my mom got religion but Lulu stayed the same, I think, stayed long hair and Joni Mitchell and Janis Joplin and peace signs, long as I've known her.

This kind of breaking heart, though, mine, it is different than when Baylor and I broke up. That was an all-over-my-skin-hurts, I-can't-move thing. Even my teeth. Like I had the flu or something. Like I needed my mother but I didn't need my mother I needed Baylor. Just to hear his name, still. All kinds of feelings. All the songs are true: the heart breaks. Because what if you can only do it once? Love. Once. Like that's all the universe lets you have. To protect you.

But turns out this is worse. I wonder now, watching Dahlia, who doesn't have to think of any of this, which makes me hate her for one second, will my heart just be breaking forever? Over and over and over again?

"I can raise this little person," I say. It doesn't come out strong at all. I don't sound like anyone's mother.

"There is more for this baby out there," Dahlia says. "If you love your baby, you have to be able to see that. Give it a future."

"Her," I say, smiling. "Not it."

"I know." Dahlia grins back at me. "You can choose it for *her*. And *she* can know who you are."

And what's so great about that, I'm thinking. Who am I?

I want time to tell me what to do. The more time I don't decide, things get decided for me. Like having an abortion. It's too late. So that's not a choice now either. It's been too long. And even if that was not the choice for me, I am not judging anyone now. We are all just trying to live through this without breaking, you know? We are all doing the best we can and I understand every one of us. I love us all. Will anyone else? Love us, I mean. Love me. Ever again. Who could?

So which one am I? The one who keeps her or the one who lets her go?

It becomes less confusing to me the more I say it, the more Dahlia says it. It is so hard to think of the future. When I saw those pink lines—the ones I jumped over into positive—I wish I could explain it. I had thought pink meant it was a girl. (Yes, seriously.) And then I have to think about what's in front of me. Baylor and I were already broken up, and I knew I could get him back with this, *this*—he is not a mean person or anything, but he so doesn't love me. And now, this growing thing. Every morning I woke up crying. I still wake up crying as soon as I remember that nothing has changed.

I need to decide.

Next to us, at the table by the window that looks out onto all the evergreens, a lady is crying. It's almost like she's doing it for both of us. She's weeping. There's a painting of bluebirds in a nest that hangs above her head and another lady reaches out and takes her hand and it feels so sweet to me I want to go over and hug them. Actually I want them to come over here and hug me. Like take me up and just make all this all go away in a way my mom isn't doing. At all.

My mom thinks what I did was wrong. It's hard for her to understand me. Believe me that goes both ways. I mean, if I had a kid, which I almost do, I would be more understanding. Baylor says he'll break up with Rosaria and marry me. He is a good guy and that is the right thing to say but that's the wrong thing to do and the reason is wrong. I know all this, but part of me—most of me—would still really like Baylor back. I would like him away from Rosaria that is for sure. My parents have money, I mean not piles of it or anything, we're not rich at all, but we're okay. We have a house and a car and growing up I had a dollhouse and a bike with a pink banana seat and roller skates with their own key. I could do this, I think. But then I think, this is no life for any of us. Least of all, you. I look down at my belly like it can hear my thoughts. Like you can. You you you. Who are you? Who will you be?

I am growing in every way I can. Someone needs to tell me the answer and it is not Baylor and please don't let it be my mother.

Dahlia is snapping her fingers at me. "Bridget!" she says in between clicks. Her nails are painted dark green and I can see the colors of them moving through space. They match the evergreens on the outside. "Let's look at more of the profiles. Maybe you haven't found the right people yet."

Do I look at her blankly?

"To give the baby to."

Give? How could I. I know Dahlia's right and I can see the answer there, waiting, delivered. One day soon I will put her in someone else's arms. I will answer someone's prayers. I will be wanting for the rest of my life. That is true love and even I know I might never get it again. Even I can see that.

"How's the letter?" Dahlia says.

I roll my eyes.

"Just say, well, whatever you want to say. About how much you love her. Because you do love her. That's why you have to let her go."

I feel the tears streaming down my face again, salt salt salt. I lick them when they reach me. Potato chip tears.

"Who told you that?"

Dahlia cocks her head. "I don't know," she says. "That's what my mother says about her first mom. You're showing a little, by the way."

I am half-disgusted; half-thrilled but I can't say it. "Now?"

"What is it? Three months?"

I nod. "And a half."

"You could start?" says Dahlia. "The letter. It could be kinda fun."

Fun? Nothing is fun anymore. I grimace.

She urges me with her head. "Writing. You could start."

I want to say: Be Brave. To both of us. Write it on this lined paper, on my skin, over my broken heart. But it's already on this stupid pen and that makes it impossible. That's what I feel, though. Be brave. Am I talking to her or to myself? Be a warrior, I want to say.

Meet me on the other side.

"Maybe you want, like, one beautiful letter that says everything," Dahlia says.

I look over at her. She is so pretty, Dahlia, like her mom. She wears makeup—really dark eyes sometimes, or even purple, which somehow works on her, I don't know how—but she also is pretty just in her Hello Kitty onesie, reading magazines next to me on the couch. I reach out to touch one of her long curls. Boing. "Boing," I say.

I crumple the blank sheet into a tight ball.

"Wait!"

"It's wrong," I say. "It's all wrong." I throw it at her.

"You can really tell now," she says softly, looking at my belly.

"Heard you the first time," I say. I am willing that part away.

My father can't look at me. At the dinner table his eyes are just fixed straight ahead. Chews his food, holds his fork in folded hands beneath his chin. Up and down, up and down. What would he even be like with her? Will he hate her or love her? I do think sometimes with boys—men, I guess—you just can't tell. Girls, we are always just on the side of love. We are. Everyone is a bird with a broken wing. Here is my wing. It is broken. It has always been broken.

Mom thinks that's because I don't go to church regularly. And that drove me to Baylor.

"I know," is what I say out loud. How can I say it? Every little thing is about this decision. One thing sways me one way, one the other. Those pink strips. I am tiptoeing along it, tightrope-walking. I can still see that moment when my life changed to this. "I can't believe I have to do this in summer."

"Baby doll dresses."

"But at least no school. I mean, no one noticed."

Dahlia gives me a side look, the one that goes with the smirk. "What?"

"People know," she says quietly. "Come on."

I don't say anything. Of course they know. I know that. I just was pretending. I was pretending that when this goes away it will never have existed at all. It won't even be gone by the time school starts.

I look down. It's still cool enough for boots—Docs—and I can still see the tips of my toes. I wriggle them in my hot boots. My feet are swollen. I feel myself becoming someone else. I am growing and growing. I want to stop it; it's too fast for me. I want to kneel down and pray; I want the answer there, on some altar, our altar, where once I used to stand and sing, where once a pastor touched my forehead with water. There it is, my answer, maybe the Lord is telling me, maybe I can see it there, my answer.

Maybe I was born a sinner and maybe this little person was sent to save me.

From what?

"Baby doll dresses and long sweaters," Dahlia says and already I am dreaming.

If only, I'm thinking. But if only what? If only what. That is what I want to know.

IVY

This is what she gave me: a quilt stitched with roses, the fabric stiff as cardboard, never washed, packed away. A pink dollhouse, new and shining; inside it there are so many rooms. And inside those rooms is wooden furniture: chair, couch, bed, television, bookshelf, sink. How many times did I rearrange all this? Slide the beds to the living room, TV in the library. Bathtub in the bedroom. But it's all the same because it's so easy and light to move pretend stuff around. And the rooms aren't real anyway.

A photograph that I have pasted into a silver locket. I keep it on a string in a jewelry box and I wear it around my neck when I am angry. I have a letter, that came with me. Proof of purchase, I guess. I have all the things that say: You were not abandoned, you were not left, you are special, you got chosen.

Your parents are the parents who raised you from the moment she left you.

When she was sixteen. I am sixteen now. Patrick's band, the Farewells, played last fall in the backyard beneath a striped yellow tent, in case of rain. It rained. It always rains here. "We are the Farewells," the lead singer, Alex, said into the mic at the beginning of the set. So serious but no one was listening.

Deviled eggs and cheese fondue. Buckets of lemonade. The Farewells and their flasks of whiskey, their earnest punk pop. Claire with a bottle of Coke in each patch pocket of her dress.

Sweet sixteen. My moms came out and danced like it was the wedding they never had. Our dogs ran in circles and sneaked table scraps until they passed out beneath the food carts.

I am grateful for my life. I wouldn't want it another way, to be someone else. But you wonder, about everything. Who else could I be? Anyone, really. It could have gone any other kind of way, which is a weirdness I can't get over.

Sometimes I admit I want the her of her; on the bad days it doesn't just sit there, it becomes me, the way I want to know. All the possibilities. Those days the words sting more: the ones you don't know about. Like when I overhear the lead singer of Patrick's band, Alex, refer to his little brother as an idiot and then, he says, he's so got to be adopted. There is no way that kid is related to me.

I mean, I'm right here. Alex? I think those kinds of words matter.

People: Don't say "gay" to describe something dumb. And don't say "adopted" to say someone's dumb either. All of us, we can hear you.

We are right here.

The photo, an *actual* photo you can hold: my moms and my birth mom and me, this little package with a red face wrapped up in a blanket with the faintest pink and blue stripes. There I am at the center. I am the prize. I have never not felt that way. Like the most-ever-wanted prize. The photo hangs on the wall by the stairwell, along with photos of my moms and my grandparents, and everyone as a child. The grandparent children photos are most remarkable to me because they're, like, colored in. There is one of Gram up there, and she's got this mass of black hair and she's only a year old. And her huge blue eyes are shaded actual blue. And then this colored-in pink lipstick. It's bizarre. That and the photo of my grandpa Harry, who I never met, playing tennis at Columbia University in a V-neck sweater—those are my favorites.

In the photo with my birth mom you can just see the side of her face—you can't really see her so well but it looks as if she's been through some kind of a war. Her hair is all over the place, like she'd woken up from thrashing to nightmares. There's a streak of purple in it. The eye that you can see in the picture is swollen, or maybe that's just how her eyes are. I never knew her, after. She wears a hospital gown. There's a plastic bracelet around her right wrist. It might say her name or it might say my name. How would I know the difference? Is there a difference anymore?

But you can't tell who she is from the picture. Like, what would she be wearing on the outside? Little tight skirt, overalls, maxi dress. You can't tell what she'd put on to become herself. What kind of a girl she is. She's just *young*. Insanely. To be a mom, I mean. The age I just became.

We have the same mouth, though. I can see even from half of it what her whole smile might look like.

My moms are dressed like my moms. Mom looks so pretty. Her hair is all black then and cut blunt, straight as a razor blade slashed across her chin. She has the loveliest hair, shiny and straight. Not like mine. I only look like me, though no one would ever notice it. I move my hands like they do now. I smile when they smile. We laugh at a lot of the same things.

But not everything. And I laugh totally different. I have never heard anyone with my laugh. Patrick, I say, tell me what I sound like.

"You," he says.

"Well, I want to sound like someone," I say, and he doesn't get it.

Where do I get these eyes, then? Gray blue. I think they look empty. Moms have dark eyes, both of them.

So I have the rough quilt and the dollhouse, but sometimes I think the only thing I got from her really was that mouth, these features. The me of me but not the I.

This is what I look like: dark hair, just a little wavy. White skin, porcelain doll–style on good pretty days, but bad in the sun on all the days. The eyes. They're a little too far apart if you ask me, but on the flip side, I have cheekbones people like to comment on. As in: cheekbones higher than the Alps, which is what my New York City gram always tells me. My Atlanta grandmother has never mentioned them at all.

In the photo Mom is wearing a sleeveless collared shirt and her arms are thin and lovely. She's looking at me like I might have hung the moon. Mo is behind her, and her light hair is cut close to her scalp. It's not gray yet. So many freckles splashed across Mo's face. Mom's more serious. Always.

No one is looking at my birth mom. Not even me.

Me! Teeny as a loaf of bread everyone looks like they want to devour. A loaf they know they can't slice up to share.

All the photos.

So some days it's okay that I have never heard my laugh on someone else, or that she disappeared before I was even a year old. Totally disappeared—no more contact at all. Look, I know things are hard for all of us. I mean, my friends are sad and angry and some don't know who they are, really, on the inside. Claire is none of those things. She, like, came out fully formed. She does what she wants. Or that's what it seems like to me, as I'm never as sure of myself. How do you *know* you want to go to sleep now, for instance? How do you know you want a long bath and not a quick hot shower? I just don't know. Patrick, I think, is more like me. He's got these hippie parents who accept everything he does. They float about him. There is a lot of amaranth and patchouli around.

For me, there's also this extra added part. Of not knowing. Of all the maybes. Could have beens. The feeling I might have been erased and drawn back into life by someone who doesn't know my face.

The story is not that complicated. It is either I was wanted or unwanted. My story is I was left behind or I was stayed with. I mean, I know, as in, I've been told, that my birth mother loved me so much she let me go. She chose them and they chose her and they chose me and we all had this choosing thing that made us us.

So what would have happened if she'd kept me? I would be a different girl. What would she be? Who? It is the strangest thing. To know this. To wonder about this world that almost was. The almost of me, the I that never was. And then: the me I became.

Why did she hand me over in the end? What did I do that was so bad? Was it when I was inside her or when I came out?

That is what it feels like on bad days. On good, normal days it's just: she was a mess. She was a kid. I would have returned me, too. I can't even keep a goldfish alive. That is a horrible story, my goldfish story, for another time. But can you imagine? When I think like that, yeah, it makes tons of sense. Find the people who are you but a million times better.

Anyway, that's not how the story ended. It ended with the three of us. Me, Mom, and Mo. There are ten million photos now. All digital. Girl triangle. The beach. Hiking. Me graduating from nursery school, kindergarten, middle school. High school will be in two years. One, two, three, four candles, all blown out. There's one photograph with her, too. Maybe I'm a year old, standing, wintertime, hat and gloves and big puffed coat. She is kneeling down and holding my hands. But still, I can't see her face.

All the photos, so many years of us, a better, bigger life. Pets and parties and school and tutors and piano lessons and ballet and ice skating and sometimes theater and restaurants and vacations on the beach, in the mountains, and pretty dresses. I am lucky; I am special. In a way it's more and in a way it's less but no matter what, I am always holding on to these two things at once, these two stories, these two ways of seeing things, and I can't say I'll ever really know if I was lost or if I was found.

So there is a quilt, a dollhouse, a few photographs, and, also, there is a letter.

Here. In my journal, pressed tight as a flower. I bring it out more since my birthday, run my hands along the careful bubble script. A child's letter. To another child. Only sometimes, just to touch it and wonder.

You, she calls me. *You.*

Now I run my hands across the letter. She pressed down hard; the paper still rises up around the ink. It feels like she meant it.

But does anyone know? Were you lost or were you found? Tell me.

Exactly.

IVY

Since my sixteenth birthday party, for these six months, I can't lie, it's just been on my brain. Fore fronted. Not pushdownable.

But today is when I show the letter and the photo to Claire.

We are hanging out in my room listening to Mazzy Star because, sadness and the nineties, I love you. Red walls, my shit's everywhere. It looks like I've been robbed. Flannels hanging off my bureau, Kurt Cobain smoking over my bed. Dragonfly lights like icicles lining where the wall meets the ceiling. Photo-booth strips of Patrick and me at the lake, goofing. Claire and me, too, Claire's nose red and peeling, me, SPF 50 white. Claire's freckles. Postcards of something from all the places I have been: paintings from the Louvre and the Musée d'Orsay, Anne Frank's house, the Colosseum. The *Mona Lisa*, The *Lilies*. Rembrandt in his floppy hat. Starry, starry nights. Hamilton Stars. Orphan Annie (adopted). Superman (also adopted). Anne of Green Gables (also . . .). The Magic Clock. Palm trees. Little squares hung that add up to things I have loved and seen and watched and heard and wanted.

So, the photo first. Because Claire is always looking at photos.

She's the art director of the school lit mag, *Crossroads*, where I am the lit editor. I got her the job this year when the senior who had it for two years graduated and now, between the two of us, we see every angsty poem and every bloody Goth pen and ink that moves through this school. Also, she collects postcards and books of these oddities—boys dressed as girls, and also terribly disturbing images of babies dressed and laid out after they've died.

"I've seen this," she says of my photo. "You've shown me. Another girl in the mix." She's putting on lip gloss, looking in the mirror.

"It's her," I say as if I don't hear her.

But Claire already knows the story. Sometimes I go months without even thinking about it. About what happened to her, all the things I don't know about what it means to disappear. That adds to the story, I think. That once she was here and then she was gone. Like a story on a story on a story. A layer cake, tower-high, frosting jammed in between.

"The third girl." She kisses the mirror.

"Claire!" I go to wipe it off with a tissue but it's just smudged up now.

I look to you and I see nothing, I look to you to see the truth, sings Mazzy S.

"Sorry." She giggles.

"Third?" I ask, tossing the Kleenex. "Girl?"

"In, like, the fifties, when girls all lived together in big cities, two roommates would advertise for a third girl. I've got a book of these photos of single girls living in these special hotels for girls and also in these little apartments in the city and it's awesome."

Who would want a book about that? Claire, I guess. I don't know. "Why?" I ask.

"Why what?"

"What's so awesome about it?"

"I don't know," she says. "They're all dressed so well, so sharply and fifties. But where are they going? They were, like, born too soon. They couldn't go anywhere yet."

That I get. I think of my grandmother. She went to college and could have had a whole career. She, like, went to law school. But she never practiced law or anything; she says she did it so she could talk to my grandfather, who was a lawyer, too. What would it have been like if all the women had become lawyers?

So Claire and this art stuff and plus she's a runner. We used to run track together but I gave it up because I hated the long distance. Claire could run forever. It doesn't even register. Me, I sprint and then I just lose my lung power. Not to mention my leg power.

Also? Claire draws.

Sketching, she says. Be still.

"Big cities," I say. "Sure." I'm about as rural as we get out here. Nowheresville, as Gram says.

I stare at the picture. There are four girls here. But the split goes three three three three. Like me, Mom, Mo. Or Mom, me, her. Or the three of them. The three moms. Maybe the third girl is me.

Or there could just be two. Me and her. No additional roommate required.

Anyway, there are other things. Patrick and winter and the
Take Themselves Oh So Seriously Farewells, and *Crossroads*.

But this is on my mind now, it's like it's growing and growing.
Part of the layers, Mo has told me. Sixteen and loved you so big
but how can you do it right at sixteen? Can't even take care of
yourself. With this I take issue but I don't say it. Love so big she
had to let you go. We wanted you and wanted you and wanted
you and would have waited for eternity until she chose us. She
chose us. We were also chosen, is what Mo always says.

I chose you, I have always wanted to tell them. On my best,
happiest days. On those days I know I did and there was purpose to the choosing. My heart chose them. Sometimes I love
Mo more and sometimes Mom. They say love is big enough to
love us both. It's not finite. In that there is no science. But isn't
there? It's hard to love them both the same at the same time. But
I know I chose them.

After the first time Patrick and I kissed—on a walk along a
gorge, fall trees bursting around us—he gave me this book about
the butterfly effect. He had seen a movie about it and how the
flapping of wings on one corner of the world can alter the flight
of another somewhere far away. His card said *In praise of that
butterfly*.

That's what this is, too. Who else could have taken me? I
could be anyone. Anyone could be my parent.

"I want to find her," I say, which surprises me because I don't
know that I've thought this yet, for certain.

Claire says, "Of course you do."

I'm silent.

"How could you not?" she asks.

"I know," I say, but I've never really felt the need until I turned sixteen and just imagined being her age. Every day I imagine it. "But you can't go back from it. Or unknow it. I always thought I'd wait until I was older."

"Let's do it!"

There she goes, Claire, just knowing. But I'm still, bath or shower, not sure yet. Don't even know if I'm *tired*.

I think of the letter, her letter. Her big, careful handwriting, how hard she pressed down, how tight she must have held that pen. How much she wanted those words to stay on that page, forever.

"Do you want to ask your parents?" Claire asks. "Maybe we can all do it together. I mean, if you want help."

I love Claire, my friend from and for a million years. Sometimes I wonder if she would choose me now—Claire got way cooler than I did. But she's as close to a sister as I'll ever get. I am for her, too, I think—she's got two brothers. Sandwiched in.

I guess when I think about it, I would like a brother or sister. To not be alone in all this. But all this can be different stuff for everyone.

For Claire? I don't know yet. She likes that I'm her weird Martian friend, adopted, two moms (the third girl), lives in the sticks. Super rural. I know that makes her love me more. Or just love me still.

If there's anyone I want to bring to meeting my birth mom,

it's her. Third girl. Claire. Long dirty-blond braid down her back. She's wearing it fishtail-style today, but I can tell she did it yesterday and it's frizzed. Bangs across her forehead. Full eyebrows. She acts like she never touches them, but I have seen her with those tweezers. She has a brow game, promise.

"I could. They wouldn't mind, I don't think, but it would mean *discussing* it," I say.

"Oh God."

"And *processing* it."

"No."

"And talking about why I want to find her now. Then Mom would cry and Mo would tell me how I am the light of their lives and they will help me do whatever I want. In anything. Be anything, they'll say, and it will all go so off topic I can't even." I think about it. "Really," I affirm, "I just can't."

"No, no, no." Claire is laughing, slapping her knees. "But I gotta say, it will save you a lot of time. Talking to your moms. How else will we look?"

I don't mention the few times in the wee hours of the night, those dark, strange *feeling* hours, I tried to find her online. Over Christmas and then again, just when it turned to the new year. Brand new. But there is nothing there. Not that I could find. No footprint at all. I don't mention the adoption registries I've hovered over, scared to give my contact information. The Facebook pages for adoptees. I just can't bring myself to press send. You can't unsend a sent message, now can you?

I half groan and fling myself facedown on my bed. I flip over and prop myself on my pillows and look at Claire, twisted around at my desk, her arm slung over the back of the chair. "Okay," she says. "I know. I can stay for dinner and we can just ask them. It can come up, like, totally randomly. Casual."

Interesting. If Claire is there, how crazy can it be? How much emotion can there be, how many questions? "That's a good one."

"I could be doing a family portrait while you're all talking."

"No thanks," I say. The last time Claire tried to draw Patrick and me it was a three-hour nightmare and we all got into a massive fight.

Claire's right hand disappears inside her fisherman sweater, like she's trying for a moment to disappear. I watch her shoulder go up, all hunchback like. Then she straightens. There she is again. Hi.

"Maybe," I say. I can't tell if they'll be into it, Mom and Mo, or if they'll be even more hurt. "We can try to talk to them. Or see how it goes anyway." We do everything at dinner here. It's like our own personal town hall over pasta and Mom's sprouted wheat bread.

I feel bad. Am I choosing Claire? Over my moms? Over Patrick? Everything is a choice. Everything is yes or no or not that one or that one, certainly. What just *happens* on its own? Just dying, far as I can tell. Choosing is exhausting. And the rest of my life is just going to be choosing more things.

Anyway, Claire's already whipping out her phone and texting her mother.

She looks back at me. "Gonna turn up!" she says, ironically, because that's not how she talks, at all.

I pick up the letter again. I hold it out to Claire but I am really holding on to everything. Everything all at once.

"Here," I say. "Her letter." Because I have never shown it to anyone.

Claire turns back toward me, reaching out her hands.

BRIDGET

April 2000

My mother comes up from behind me while I'm putting on lip gloss and says, "No." That's all she says. "No."

She is so pissed. I mean she's trying to be cool about it, I guess, just to make sure we go through with it. She has bought me some cute clothes already to show that she's being supportive. I take one look at these jeans with their massive little pouch in the front, some serious nerding out, though I will say it reminds me of a kangaroo and here you are my little joey all packed up tight inside. Hi, I think, looking down at the you that is protected by the total geek that is now me.

Only of course, of course, it won't be mine by then. We will be handing it over to these people, I think. I think I think.

"Baylor," I say because I still want him to be here for this with me. I don't want him with Rosaria; I want us to be together forever, when we can have babies of our own. I mean, like, in a planned kind of way. I know that's not going to happen now, no matter what, though I do keep thinking that if I say no to all of this, maybe I can still keep him. He will have to stay. That is how it works. We will be a family. Sometimes that feels okay, but when the social worker says to me, you need to parent when *you*

want to, when *you're* ready, when *you* choose, I just think she is
trying to take her. For her business. There are a lot of people who
are choosing to be parents only it's too late for them now. There
are many more of them than there are of me. I can see how many
profiles this lady has in her stacks.

"Sit here," I say to Baylor. "Please?"

Poor Bayle. Kid has no idea what he's getting into. I don't
have those feelings like some girls do, like, well, you should have
thought of that before when we were doing it, because it was
both of us who decided. We love each other. Loved. It wasn't a
mistake. Just bad timing I guess. Poor timing, my mother calls
it. Timing and Judgment. All poor. All-against-the-Lord poor.

Now he sort of shuffles over my way. Sits down. Clueless.
I can tell he doesn't know whether he should take my hand.
Where is the place that it says *when you are about to meet the family who will be taking your child away, take the girl's hand*? There
is no handbook that says *ask for it* either. The hand. At least not
that I know about.

I don't want him to touch me because something about that
makes me feel like I will unzip and all of me will spill out. Blah.
Me. Here you go, Baylor Atkins, all my fears and memories.
Even if he just touches my shoulder. The good ones of being little and hiking with my father. Before boys. Through the woods.
Boots on soft moss. That feeling. The one where you broke up
with me at the reservoir while your friends waited for you at the
rocks. That feeling, too, Baylor Atkins.

I am desperate to be humble but I don't know that I am, not
yet. I don't know where to look. The part about being humble

I can take. That part of what my mother tells me sounds good to me.

But where is the place that tells you where to look?

Originally Baylor hadn't wanted to come today. But both our moms were like, you were there when it happened, you're sure as heck going to be there now. You need to help Bridget choose. Help me. Help me choose who this little person will grow up with. Will grow up to be. Bayle, I said to him, this person can be better than we are. She can have all the things forever and ever. Please, please, someone help me choose.

I get to pick the life you will have. Do I get to pick who you will be?

She? he said because it was only those pink lines back then.

I don't repeat what I know. In me is a girl and she is growing to be something better than all of us. She could be anything or anyone. And I could be, too. What are the dreams again? Tell me. You meet a boy and fall in love. Right? You get married? Buy a house, right? What are the dreams again?

I would be lying if I said I don't think of her sometimes, maybe older, in a really sweet little sequined tutu, hair in French braids (I can braid so well now), holding my hand as we walk, through the mall maybe, down by the reservoir and the creek. All the little stores. All the rocks sparkling from under the water. Sequins refracting light. Whatever you want, is what I want to say to her, I will buy it for you, but it's not like that is the truth. I can't even drive on my own to the mall. Learner's permit. How am I going to get her to the place where I can't even buy her anything she wants?

Will my heart be breaking forever? Like this.

Smashed.

These people today are from Phoenix. They came all this way to meet me. Are these people the best people? I have what they want: I am in school with the father who is ready to sign the papers. I am not on drugs. I am not a mermaid or a swan or a goat or a devil. I am not living in a cave or beneath the sea. I am a girl. I am only a girl. I have done things I regret—so many things, this with Baylor isn't even first on the list—but I think this thing I am about to do will take the cake and win the whole bake sale. But which is the way I will regret it more, I can't now say. To stay or go, I mean. I just can't say.

They pull up. Rental car. I wonder what their real car looks like.

I watch them look up at our door, covering their eyes from blinding sun. What are they seeing? Our little clapboard house. Those cheesy lights by the number: 3476. Eagle Pass. Means nothing, the number. Or does it mean everything? It all depends how hard I'm looking and what I'm looking for. Rickety steps, need mending. Chain-link fence. Not white and wooden, not like in the movies. Is theirs like in the movies? Show me a picture, I want to demand. Let me see your white picket fence.

It's early but I can still hold my belly and imagine I am holding it, holding her. I can wonder: What if I choose wrong? These two people here: she is tall and a little too thin, a little too white. He's all teeth. They might be good, they might have money, but does that make them right for you?

Right for us?

Baylor is checked out. Has that faraway look that makes him seem a little, well, touched. I can see him drumming his fingers on his thighs. His fingers are one of his good features. Thinking about them still makes me shivery all over. Hands are such strange things. It's amazing you are allowed to have them out in public without gloves on. They do such private, shocking things.

Baylor likes this couple because, according to the profile the agency sent us, the man played in a band about one hundred years ago. Maybe a thousand.

When I showed Baylor the profile, he had tilted his head to the side and said, "I can see me a little bit in him."

Really? I had thought. Because Baylor doesn't even play an instrument.

"I might play one day," he said. "I mean, I could. Now. I could be anything."

I get what he means. I do.

Why did I choose them? Was it the desert? Their profile showed them standing in a garden along a path lined with cactuses. Once, when I was a little girl, I went to the desert. It is the only time I ever went on a plane. I was with Dahlia, visiting her aunt, and Lulu paid for my trip. Everything was dead and alive at the exact same time. It was freezing and burnt to a crisp. It was the sun and the moon. It was so extreme I couldn't take it—but I kept thinking what would I be if I had grown up here among all these lizards and flowering cactuses?

Dahlia and I hiked into the mountains. It got dark so quickly there.

The profile said: we have a garden of cactuses and we like to hike.

So that memory came back to me. A memory of me wondering about the future. A memory of the only time I'd ever been somewhere else.

The knock is soft. Our doorbell is broken.

I open the door and there they are, smiling fake and wide and looking down at me. They hand me a stuffed bear, but who is that really for? A stuffed bear is for a baby. I won't have one. Remember? You will be taking mine. The bear is really for yourselves. It's yours.

I open the door. I take the bear. It smells like a rental car, stale and sugary. No part of me wants to let these people in.

"Sit down," my mother says. "Please." My mother in her mom jeans and bad mall shirt and her chalky pink lipstick. Hard to imagine my mother hanging out and listening to Janis Joplin while her and her best friend's boyfriends were at a war, like Lulu says. My mom never talks about any of that.

Anyway, I've never felt so strange. Once my father sold my bike when I stopped riding it. He put an ad on Craigslist and some people came by to look at it. I watched them from my window, examining this bike with its white basket, those old plastic flowers and the bell that was rusted from the time I left it out in the rain. I was always leaving that bike out in the rain. My father crossed his arms as the people ran their fingers over the pink banana seat. Ten bucks. A man opened his wallet and handed my father the cash and there went the bike to another person's daughter.

Mrs. Arizona has a name. It's Esme. Isn't that beautiful? She doesn't know I've chosen them because of the cactuses and because of her name. It's beautiful but it doesn't look like her. She is harder than I thought. Sharper. Her edges, she's all sticks and stones, but not the kind you can build nests with.

My mother sits, too. She doesn't ask them if they want anything to drink and I guess why should she.

Mr. Arizona is Matthew. He's all teeth and you can see them because he's smiling. Deranged smiling. He looks at Baylor, at a chair next to the couch, and Baylor smiles back at him, looks down.

I bet he's thinking, this guy played in a *band*? That's what I'm thinking anyway.

"We want to do whatever makes you most comfortable," Esme says when we settle in a bit. She seems to be talking to me and my mother, which is annoying. Because it should just be me. "We want you to visit if you want, you can stay with us. Pictures every few months. Whatever level of openness you want." Again, she looks at my mother.

I nod, as loudly as possible. "I don't really know yet," I say. I imagine staying in their house. Like, in some guest room, my daughter down the hall in a room of her own. Not my daughter anymore. "Pictures sound really good." I imagine it. "And cards," I say. "Like valentines."

They nod. I sound like an idiot but I don't care because I do want a valentine, one that spills out glitter and sparkles and pink feathers when I open it.

"Well, ask us anything," Esme says. "Please. We want to be as open with you as possible." She takes Matthew's hand and sort of stretches it into her lap. It seems disconnected from Matthew now. Like it's just Esme's. He doesn't seem to love it but he can't say anything because he knows I must be watching for anything that makes them seem less than perfect. And I am.

I want to ask about the cactuses. They flower in the wintertime, don't they? I want to ask. That sounds pretty to me.

I want to ask about the room they will make for her. What color will it be? I think yellow is nice. How big is it? Will there be a turtle that shines stars onto the ceiling like I once saw in a movie? A mobile that spins and plays lullabies? Soft blankets and teddy bears? I want to ask all these things because suddenly I realize these people have to be 1,000 percent better than me. Otherwise, *why*? Because what if I choose wrong. What if they are worse? What if they fight or go out all the time or leave her alone in a restaurant or a hot car with closed windows? What if it should have been me all along?

What if I am being tested?

My heart is racing. I had thought, I will just know. It will all be so clear. But it is not clear. This is all wrong.

My mother looks at me and I look out into the kitchen. My mom and I used to make muffins together on Sunday. Morning glory muffins, with raisins and carrots and coconut. When did we stop? A while ago now. I can't think of the last time we did anything together. And I am still hers.

"It doesn't have to be now," Esme reassures me. "We can keep in contact and you can call with questions you think of. Whenever."

I nod.

She takes a wrapped box out of a shopping bag. *Williams-Sonoma* it says in green type. Never heard of the place but it seems uptight.

She nods at me, basically pushing me to open it.

She seems pretty happy about her gift, but I know, I just know, that inside the box is not anything I want.

The box is wrapped in brown paper, like a grocery bag, and it is tied with ribbed green ribbon, which matches the shopping bag. I untie the green ribbon. I tear through the paper. Everyone watches me. I catch Baylor eyeing me, too.

"It's a juicer!" Matthew says. He can, like, barely contain his excitement.

Well, I'll be, that riddle has been solved, I think as I watch my mother pretend to be totally thrilled. "Ooh, yes," she says. "Wonderful!"

I set it down on the carpet.

"So you can be sure to have enough fruits and veggies," Esme says, looking at my stomach. "So you can be healthy."

Me? You mean the baby. It is getting confusing already. They don't love me; they won't love me. Do I want their love? Do they think I will feed this baby, I don't know, bug spray and Windex?

I can't. I feel like I'm going to either pass out or laugh like the homeless lady on the Commons in town, or just throw up. I stand, woozy. My mother eyes me. Sit down, she says with her eyes. They turn to slits. You sit down right now.

I sit down. "Thank you," I say to the Phoenix, Arizonas.

"Of course," Esme says, her husband nodding maniacally

behind her. "We would love to provide you with more stuff . . . for the baby, I mean, when you decide we're matched. If, I mean. If we're matched."

The counselor has told me: matched is when you hook up with the right family. She's told us: I'm the birth mom. And my baby is suddenly an adoptee. Which makes me feel like she won't have a leg or something. "Thanks." Well, this is awkward, I'm thinking, as I press my hands between my knees. "That's so nice." I start nodding a lot, too. I can feel it but I can't stop.

And there goes my mother with her mean eyes again.

Baylor has basically sunk into himself. No one seems to see him.

Michael says, "Our lawyer has an account where you can draw money for things you need." He looks over at my mother, who is nodding furiously. "Rent, for instance." He looks around the room.

What does he see? I wonder. The cracked ceiling? The dirty walls? The bad eighties wall-to-wall carpet?

"Thank you," I say.

"And pretty maternity clothes. And groceries," Esme adds, smiling.

I feel like this hour will last an eternity but then, after that and some discussion of the school system in Phoenix and also the golf there, and all the aunts and cousins in their lives and all of this but nothing about the cactuses, finally, it's over.

I stand up when they do and I let them hug me, all their corners digging into my softening places, and I let them touch my stomach and push at my hair and I let them, for that day, think that this baby will be theirs. They want her. I am not on drugs and, look, I have a mother right here and she's normal enough, and Baylor, he's saying, please, take this baby so I can be with my new hot girlfriend and not feel too crappy about it, please, and there aren't a lot of red flags, that's what the counselor calls them. There are no red flags here. It's not a favor to them, me letting them believe for this one day. I don't know how else to do it. And also I don't know how to undo it.

What if I hadn't waited so long? To decide. I mean, what if I had peed over that stick earlier, if those lines hadn't divided my life—before I took the test and after. What if I had just snuck off and gotten rid of it and never said a word to anyone?

If only I had just a little bit less. Or a little bit more. The decision would be easier then, right?

These people, they came all this way. They got on a plane and they probably held hands and squeezed tight and said, this is it this is it this is the one. But I want to feel that, too. Even if nobody is here to hold my hand.

What, I wonder, as they get up to leave, does it really mean to Be Brave?

IVY

I watch Claire unfold the letter. I've memorized it by now, but I read over her shoulder, like I'm reading it from Claire's brain, not mine. I don't expect it, but she begins to read it out loud.

October 25, 2000
Dear You,
I call you Lily I call you Lilac I call you Daisy and Tulip and Heather and Dandelion and Rose. But I named you Ivy: climbing, strong, ever green. We are going to grow together, okay? Okay? Even apart, whatever your name becomes, we're still together. You are in my heart tonight. I am your mother but Joanne and Andrea are your mothers for real. When I met them I felt like I had already seen them before. I recognized them. I don't know if you can believe it but that is the story. Immediately in my heart, I felt they were family and that there were forever kinds of love. I knew they were your parents. I will not lie. That was sad for me. Do you know how much they wanted you? High as the sky big as the world. God did his job. You saved my life. You snatched me from the dark. And you saved your parents. Seven years they were

waiting. I think of it that we all answered each other's prayers.
That is a miracle. You are a miracle. Letting you go is the
hardest thing I have ever done. It is the saddest thing. I am waiting
for the sweetness of you to swallow the bitterness of the not you. You
are going to be amazing. Always remember that I love you with all
of my heart that is so big now, since you've come into the world.
Now we both have to be brave.

Love,
Your first mom

I have read the letter a million times but today it sounds like
it's Claire saying the words. It's too strange that it could be anyone. I have never heard her voice. I blink back new tears.

She folds the letter back up. "That's such a sweet letter. I can't
believe you haven't shown it to me," she says. She hands it back
and I quickly put it inside my journal, that secret pressed-flower
place. Claire's arms alight, fold into themselves. Disappearing
wings.

"I guess." I look back at her. I shrug. It doesn't really say a
thing, does it? It tells me nothing but that, well, she could spell.

"I can't imagine," she says. She rubs my back at the open space
between my shoulder blades, where I imagine I once had wings.
When were they taken from us? Our wings.

"Thanks," I say. I turn the dragonflies on and off and then on
again. Blink. Blink. Blink.

Blink.

She goes back to the mirror and leans in, tries to rub off her lip gloss. "It's so much to think about."

I nod. But she's looking at herself.

"I want to have something perfect to say but all I can think is I'm starving," she says. "When's dinner anyway?"

BRIDGET

April 2000

I go to my bedroom mirror that's perched on my old scratched-up dresser, thrift-shop smudges at the corners. I can hear the Phoenix, Arizonas walking away. I know it's for the best. I won't choose them. My skin is breaking out around my hairline. I tried some cornstarch to soak up all the grease but that was just clumpy and then I tried a new kind of gel but those red dots are still there. I want to prick them with a needle, see what's in there. What's in there? It can't be good.

My nose is dry and red from a cold I've had since week three of this. Everything good goes to the baby they say. They is: doctors, nurses, my mother when she's not so pissed she can't look at me. My father, that's different. He's mostly sad about it. It's like they've switched. My angry vet dad is sad and my mom is the one ready to shoot. Oh, Valerie, I hear myself think. That's my mother. Valerie. Happy Valley we called her back when we joked together, my dad and me, the few times the same things made us laugh.

Anyway, it's like all the good from my food (Is there any good in Hot Pockets? Because that is all I want to eat . . .), all the good from my body goes to the baby. Left behind is what's for me. And there's nothing left. Already she is taking and taking and taking. That's what kids do, is what my mother has been telling me her whole life. Take it all.

"They were nice!" my mother is at the door, leaning in. I can tell she doesn't really believe it either.

"Seriously? A juicer?" I turn toward her.

"Well," she says. "They brought something."

"A teddy bear?"

"You need to get a job." She walks in, swiping the dresser with her finger. "And you need to clean," she says as she flips her finger over to see the fingerprint of dust.

"Seriously?"

"Bridget," my mother says.

"Mom!" I look down at my belly and back up at her again. "Don't you want to be a grandma?"

She looks at me like she will wring my neck. "You need to choose a family for this child and you need to get a job."

"How am I going to work at the pool again? Come on, be real."

Last summer I taught swimming to little kids at the public pool. There was a boy there named Nelson, the head lifeguard. That was before Baylor. I couldn't wear a bikini to camp—you can't teach kids in a two-piece apparently—and I remember lying out in one of our free swims in this one piece, and the feel of the sun on me, baking, Nelson twirling his whistle, seated above all those screaming kids. I remember shielding my eyes, all the bright light and dark in them when I sat up to look at Nelson looking at me.

This summer. A bikini. I want to scream at my mother, about all of it. What if it could all be in there, in one scream?

"So don't work at the pool," she says. "But work somewhere."

I am not getting the support that the agency says I need. I mean, where is the understanding here? There is just this pissed-offness. "Really? Did you just say that?" I want to scream more at her. But what can I say? I need my mother.

She turns to me. "A job will help, Bridget," she says. "Keep busy."

I need to be inside. Something inside and hidden where no one can see me.

"A family," she says.

"Aren't we a family?" I ask.

She stiffens. "We are already a family. The baby needs parents," my mother says. I see her, like, break a little bit. "I can help you," she says. "Look through those pamphlets."

"They're profiles," I say.

"Do you need help?" She scratches her ear. It's such a random gesture. "Choosing the right ones, I mean."

I shake my head. "That's okay," I say. I can't really bear to search for her mother with my mother. It's too sad.

What I need is to decide.

"I'm here," she says.

I hear her go downstairs and I look back. Here I am in this mirror. A mess. I face myself. I am a girl who just met these people who are not going to take my baby. Who are they saving? Who am I saving. What does that even mean anymore?

They have to know, I think. That I won't be calling. But

if I do, then what else will they send me? What will the next wrapped-up box be?

I go to the kitchen and call Dahlia to meet.

"Not the reservoir," I say to Dahlia. "Everyone will be there today."

"How about the creek?" No one goes to the creek in the day. The creek is something to hop for the woods at night. Which is why I like it now.

I'm there first. I take off my boots and socks and stand in the water. It's warm but this creek is always so cold. Used to be crayfish in here but not anymore. Everything in this town is dead or dying. Imagine, imagine, I am thinking here: maybe I could have been a person who does not care about saving anyone. I try not to think about the pastor and my mother with her hands on her hips. I just want this to be me, choosing; I want it to be a secret I can keep.

Dahlia appears, suddenly and softly beside me. She kneels down and takes off her Converse. I think for a minute what we look like. Two girls in cold water, holding up the ends of our dresses. But we have all this other stuff inside us.

This place, this little ribbon of cold, clean water, it's like a secret before the woods. I wonder now why I never spent any time here, just jumped over hoping to get to wherever I was going.

Then.

I got my hands in my pockets and I feel the pen, run my thumb and finger along it, smooth to sharp. *Be Brave.* Dahlia runs her hands—her green nails are dots like fish in the spring—in the cool water. I lean down, too. Place my hands on chilled rocks, the cold, cold water, let the bottom of my dress skim the surface. You can hear Butterpeak Falls from here, the sound of rain but no rain at all.

"My mother says I need to get a job," I say. "Like you, I guess."

Dahlia works scooping ice cream in town. It's made her hands practically arthritic but she can't stand ice cream now, which seems like a good thing to me. She nods.

I look into the spring sun, that bright, clear, just-warm-enough sun, and I am looking for the answer. When I was little I dreamed on this water, made my wishes here at this creek. Always saw my own reflection, cracked by coins and buttons. Cracked open. Rippled. It's a little like that now.

"If only," I say, but it's like Dahlia has stopped listening.

Or maybe I have. It's me. There is my blue sky above. I hardly ever look up. I pull at the hair on my arms. I'm here.

"Tell me about Mr. and Mrs. Phoenix, Arizona."

I am thinking of a boy who would give up his heart. Now my dreams and wishes have to be something different.

When I get home my mother will say again how that was so freaking fabulous about the juicer, don't you think, Bridge? She will say you are being good and bright and hopeful and you are having faith you are laying yourself at the altar like you need to. The answer, she will say, it is surely written there.

I think for a second about getting on some bus to anywhere and just going somewhere now, near the ocean maybe. Or a big city. Either place, you can disappear there.

I feel my pen. *Be Brave.*

Dahlia puts her arm around me and I lean into her.

Phoenix, Arizona. All the cactuses and coyotes and setting suns. It's just so far away.

IF ONLY

Arizona

"I'm coming!" I call out to my grandmother but I have no intention of going toward the house. She gets scared of the bats but I like to come watch them and the white moths feed off the cactuses, sucking out the nectar just as the flowers start to open at twilight. Night in my mother's garden doesn't scare me.

I think our cactus garden is my favorite place. My mother planted most of these before I was born, before they met me as they like to say, and before, as my father says, anything mattered to them. The sky, now, it's like a velvet painting here, all pinks and oranges and red, almost cheesy, totally unreal, and the cactus flowers—the organ pipe and senita (yes, I know their names, all of them) —are just opening. They're ten feet high and they line the walk that leads out of our garden and out onto the street. Also: prickly pear and beavertail cacti, the fishhook barrel I stepped on once when I was a toddler. That is one of my first memories: stepping on a cactus.

The smell: like vanilla and the wind and the moon.

The second memory is blowing out the candles on my third birthday cake, my mother leaning in behind me.

My mother is surely here in this garden if she is anywhere.

"Sage! Now!" I hear my grandmother calling me.

I linger out here tonight. Maybe I am calling ghosts. We all know it's the anniversary, but no one says it. Five years is a long time. I have been without a mother twice.

Two times I've been left behind.

But what I'm thinking about is driving out of town with Raven. It was just last month and it was dark, 10:00 p.m., but not so late that it was strange to be out, and we were driving toward the preserve. Even though I can't remember the reason why we were heading out there now, the night is unforgettable to me. The clock on R's dash glowed 10:13. The street was empty but the streetlights were shining and all the saguaros along the side of the road and the buttes rising up from the valley were silhouetted against the sky. R was saying she needed to get home, which made me look at the clock again. Now it said 11:07 but we hadn't been riding for more than ten minutes. We hadn't done a near hour's worth of distance, that much I know.

The streetlights began to shut off, one by one, just as we passed them, as if it was our car that switched them off. Then, behind us, a trail of darkness. The lights on the dash started flashing and then flickered out. Our cells powered down. The temperature dropped inside of the car and it was like we were sailing beneath moonlight only.

We didn't say anything, just held our breath, waiting for something to happen. What would it be? It was just silence, like we were the only ones here on earth for one moment and then the streetlights clicked on one by one, the lights on the dash began to flash. The clock reset: 10:14. Only one minute had passed and yet we had covered far more ground than one minute would allow.

Raven stopped the car and we got out and looked up at the stars. We sat on the warm hood of the ticking car and just watched the sky like we'd done on any kind of night here. Night watching. One star shot through the night. But it seems to be there is always a shooting star if you get far enough out of town. Or perhaps it was a night of meteor showers, as shooting stars aren't really stars at all.

All my mothers, I thought then. Watching.

"Coming, Amma," I call back to my grandmother now. My grandmother who lost a daughter when I lost a mother.

I love being in my mother's garden, feel her hand in it, all the things she grew for my brother and me. I have often wondered about this hand, the one I've been dealt, the one where all the moms get taken.

So was it a ghost? That's what I asked Raven then on the hood of that car, lying back, watching our particular square of sky on our particular planet, and later, when we got home, and, still, now, we are trying to understand it.

We weren't scared. We aren't scared. This is our world.

Is this a ghost story?

I jump when I feel Amma's warm hand on my shoulder. "It's getting dark," she says.

I turn around and the house glows behind me. All the warm rooms I have looked out of and watched the sun slam down from in this moonlike world.

But I am carrying this with me now. The story of the dark

road, the messed-up clock, the cold interior. The story of my first mom and then the next. All the streetlights flashing dark then light again.

I let my grandmother take me by the hand, lead me inside for dinner. Her hand is dry and powdery and thick with calluses.

If this is not a ghost story, I don't know what is.

IVY

2017

This is what we do: Every morning we go down to the chicken coop and get the eggs. Picking eggs is my favorite. Took me a while to get used to the smell but the warmth in there, and then the warm eggs, I just love it. There are goats, too. Mo makes cheese for all our neighbors, who live miles away. Mom is a city person turned country and Mo is country but from the south. Sometimes it's a thing between them. How Mom grew up and how my grandmother comes out to see us with leather boots from Bergdorf's, soft as a baby's cheek, and little pastel-colored cakes from Bouchon, smoked salmon and gravlax and onion bagels from Russ & Daughters, just like my grandfather loved, I'm told.

But that's another story. I bring it up now just because of dinner: pork carnitas. Flour tortillas, the tomatillo salsa Mom canned last summer. We're on the deck, which is pretty, really dark wood, Mo actually sanded it herself *with no help from Mom* as she tells pretty much anyone new to the deck, and it's late enough spring that the trees are all full and green and swaying but the deranged bugs haven't started biting yet. We're on the lake. From May through October it's pretty wonderful here.

Our dogs, two rescues—Court and Spark, and I never call them adopted—are all seated, waiting to gobble up whatever gets dropped.

Winter? The lake effect is no joke is all I can say.

Claire just starts in. "So," she says. "Hi, so." It's more to push me to talk than anything else I think.

Mo and Mom look at each other. They each have a beer in their hand, perfectly chilled as far as I can tell, and they're relaxed and easy. Dinner is a nice time in my house. I've got no complaints about dinner here.

I cut in. "So I'm sixteen," I begin. So much for just coming up in random convo. Thanks, Claire.

Mom and Mo look at each other. "Are you two getting married?" Mo says. Then she busts out laughing.

"Maybe," I say, momentarily offended, like they're the only ones with some claim to gayness. "Anyway, no." I just cut it off. "Listen. Really. So sixteen is big because, well, that's when my birth mom had me, right? That was her age, I mean."

They both go serious. Full on. I can tell it's like Parenting 101: time to pay attention. Let's be *present*. Hup, two. "Yes," Mom says, softening. "Absolutely. That was when she had you. I know birthdays can feel like happy days and they can also feel like sad days because—"

"Mom! Mom."

"Yes, sorry. Please, honey, continue."

"Well, what happened to her? Do you know?" I ask. It's not the first time or second or third, but being sixteen makes it feel different.

"I don't know." Mom shakes her head. "I've told you that, honey, many times. I'm sorry."

Mo shifts in her seat. "We don't," she says, and I can't tell if the emphasis is on the "we" or the "don't."

"We lost her just before your first birthday." Mom looks down.

"Lost her?"

"Lost track," says Mo. "Mom meant lost track."

"It was terrible. We had thought she would be in our lives. Part of our family. I mean, of course, she still is. She grew you in her tummy and—"

"Mom! God, I know the story, okay?"

"All right," my mother says. "I just want to emphasize how important she was to us."

"Is," corrects Mo.

"Nothing else, then?" I turn to Mo, who is more reasonable on these issues. "Like no other girl things?" I'm thinking of the dollhouse. "Like dolls, for the dollhouse, maybe?" I say it.

There is silence.

"No more girl things," Mo says. "We filled the dollhouse, Ivy. We bought all the furniture."

"You did?"

They nod.

"I didn't know that." I look at Claire and she looks down at her plate.

This stops me. I have always thought that my birth mother had filled it up. But it makes sense, doesn't it? She gives the house and they make it a home.

"I do wonder about her all the time," Mom says. "Every day,

I think. She gave us you. We loved her. We love her. We had thought you would know her and when she didn't show up for our scheduled meeting—you were, like, eleven months—we kept trying her. But it was as if she had vanished. Like that." Mom snaps her fingers. "I mean, she had not shown up a lot. We didn't see much of her that first year, but she always came around eventually."

"Vanished?" Claire asks.

Mo nods. "Yes, Claire," she says, and I sense a tiny bit of annoyance on her part. I wonder if she wishes Claire were not here. "She really did. And then we thought, well, this is hard for her now. We had all been so on board for this open adoption. Not everyone knew about open adoption. Not like now, where they're all that way. But here was a lot of trust there. We were very worried about her. I'd read about all that. How there can be, umm, well, regrets. It's very hard that first year. It gets easier, I've read. I'm not saying that's true for everyone, but it can get a lot easier. To manage. But now I think, you think it's going to get easier and you wait for it, and what if it doesn't? What if it gets harder?"

"Am I the 'it'?" I ask.

"I mean, well, parting with you. That is what I mean by 'it.'"

I feel that in my heart, I think. This notion of regret. What if I was living the wrong life? Like I was meant to be with her. I want to be here, though, too. Could you be both places? Like, live two lives at the same time? I consider this. Being split. And yet, I am already split.

"Like she went into a void and never came out."

Mom says, "We had been very close. I mean, we had spent time together. And spoken on the phone. We'd emailed."

For a moment I picture my moms with this girl, like, buying her clothes and maybe taking her to nice dinners. Is that how it works? I picture them watching her and listening to her, treating her body like it was golden, sort of like they do me. I am gold and glass and all things special and fragile and delicate. But that can be hard, too. On me. The delicate one. To be so strangely handled. To never ever be ignored or taken for granted or mistreated. That is a lot of focus I gotta tell you. A lot.

Mo laughs a little bitterly. "I think we were hurt. Like she'd rejected *us*."

"But it was just me she rejected," I say.

"That's not what I meant though I get why you might think that. Really, I think it must have been so hard. Ivy, I know this is difficult to hear, but I can't imagine losing you. I'm sure it hurts her. Still. Wherever she is."

Claire sits back and only then do I notice how the four of us are all on the edges of our seats, leaning into each other, like so eager to get our thoughts out.

"Wherever she is," Claire says. "Where is she?"

I watch Mo and Mom look at each other. Just a glance and then they both take a quick swig off their beer bottles. I could ignore it but I don't. Why should I? Sixteen.

"What?" I say.

"What what?" laughs Mo.

Another brief exchange between my parents. Nothing makes me feel more like an alien and when I feel that way I wonder:

Is it because I'm adopted? Does everyone feel that away about their parents? Most everything that happens that makes me feel odd or mad or outside, makes me think this. Or is it because I have no siblings? Or that my parents are gay? How do you know, though? How do you know what the thing is that your weird feelings come from?

My life exists because of a swish of that butterfly's wing. Patrick's book, a theory of chaos. Where was the swish of the flight? How far away? And what was changed? Was there a storm because of it or was the storm averted? Was it a tsunami? Have I saved the world? Or destroyed it.

It could have been anything. I could be anywhere. I could be anyone. Am I the best me possible? Of course not. I could be big city or rich as hell or one of six siblings in the woods somewhere, homeschooled, or—or with her. That is the life I can't imagine. The only one I can't see. The her of it.

But I don't say anything like this. The thoughts are constant and then they're just . . . gone. Butterfly wings. A dragon's tail. A firefly blinking in the night. Anything really.

"I thought we had no secrets in our family," is what I actually say. "I thought secrets were, like, the devil. Like Mo's family secrets almost killed her, like, Mom, you keeping being gay from Gram . . ."

"I get it," Mo says.

"Well, I feel like there is still a secret," I say. "Somewhere in here." My hands stir at the air above the table.

Mom traces her thumb along the table's rough iron. The paint is chipping a bit, just in a kind of rustic farm-like, lived-in way.

She looks up at me now, kind of dramatically. Mo nods her head at her as if to say, it's okay, go ahead.

And so she does.

"We do have a letter," Mom says. She looks at Mo.

Mo guzzles her beer. Claire's hands sprout out of her too-big sweater, ready for mad flight. I inadvertently slam my hands on the table.

"What? A letter?"

"Yes," Mom says quietly.

"You kept it from me?" I stand up for emphasis but I decide to shelve the anger for when I need it one day, for when I'm about to be grounded for lying about where I was or what I was doing and I can say, oh, right, like you kept that letter from me, you guys are the liars! Then I remember I don't really lie to them and that they really wouldn't ground me, so I decide to embrace the anger in the now instead. "For how long? Let me see it!" I demand.

Mom rises, too. "We're not keeping it from you. We were just saving it."

"For what? For, like, the day I figure out to ask for it?"

"I actually have no idea," Mo says. She shrugs. "What we were waiting for. I really don't."

She leaves and the screen door slaps three times. I always find it funny in this day and age where everything is so, I don't know, technological, and modern and steel, and then there are these things like screen doors that have been here forever and just sound like the past.

Claire and I exchange looks and then Mo comes back, not two minutes later, with a bulky envelope. She places it so carefully in my hands, like it's a delicate bird's nest, fallen from a tree.

The first thing I notice is that it's already been opened.

"It's open!" The rage grows. Who knew. I've never felt that before, not for my parents anyway. More for, like, the world and all the bad things happening in it, the cruelty to vulnerable people. To animals. I feel that a lot. It's that kind of rage, though, for a second anyway.

Next I notice the date stamp: July 28, 2012. That is a lot of holding on my moms did.

Shaking, now also from fear, I think, I dip into the envelope that has something besides a letter inside. A stone, milk white and shaped like a small egg, smooth and shiny. Mom reaches out to rub my arm and I move away. My heart sort of lurches and then I take the rock, rub it shinier with my thumb.

I look at my parents and Claire, blinking into the sun that's going down over the tree line along the ridge, one last time to blind us before morning. I look at the rock that I know has touched her. My birth mother. The letter I know she wrote. What were her hands like? I look down at mine. Like these fingers? I look at them and they just seem foreign to me.

Mo's hands are on the table tapping nervously at the edge. Broad nails, perfectly square. Short fingers, so many silver rings. The skin is wrinkling a little, crepe-like, working hands. Mo hands. My Mo. For a moment I'm just sad because I don't know what's about to happen. I look up, though, and now I'm just angry again at being lied to.

BRIDGET

May 2000

The Arizonas make me think more about the city and staying east. We're not that far but far enough away that I have only had dreams about it. What would it be to look up all the time? To have so many people around you, all kinds, to never want for anything to do? To never be bored. When I was super little I had thought I wanted to be an artist. I traced all my CD covers. Drew all kinds of animals. I liked that feeling. Of drawing and being careful. And concentrating, hard. But then I just forgot, I guess. I don't know why I stopped. This is some of what I'm thinking when Sally and Andrew, the next set of parents, the next interview, pull up.

Their car is a piece of dog doo. So there's that. Bumper sticker says Clinton-Gore but, okay, I guess, hooray for the nineties. Thankfully my mom has excused herself for the day—she doesn't like city people—and I told Baylor he didn't have to show. He hesitated and was like, it's my choice, too. You know that's my child also, don't you?

And actually, for the first time I think about how it is. His. Too. So come, then, I told him.

He looked at me. Those Baylor eyes. Like look at me as if you are a puppy and, what, I will want to pet you? What? Why do guys always look that way when they want something?

Like I said, Bayle, I'll handle it.

I don't care that it is his child really anymore but it's true, my choice matters to him. He will have a little girl in the world. Maybe, in the end, she will have those sweet eyes, too. Or that nose of his. His splash of freckles and long eyelashes. Or maybe his walk. How would that look on a girl? Is that a thing you learn or a thing you're born with? Baylor's walk: Have you ever seen a boy be so confident and so unsure at the same time? That is Baylor walking. That is Baylor in the world.

But he didn't want to come, I know he didn't, we're not in this together anymore. I've been watching the videos of birth parents from the agency and it's not me and this boy holding hands and looking at each other and the camera, both, like all the couples they've filmed. We're separate now. I get to decide. I will show him the people but he can't say yes or no. He has lost that chance. That choice.

Is that fair? I don't really care.

So here it is, just me. Dahlia, too, so she can see it and help me. It's so hard to see everything you need to see all at once. All the things: what they look like and what they say and what they mean and what they bring and what they don't bring. How they act. To me and to each other. All the things you can't tell at one time. Alone.

Let me tell you this: The people have to be spectacular. All the things I'm not is who they have to be. If it's not going to be me or

Baylor and me in our fake love or me and my mom or just me on my own with my little partner in life here, then it has to be something wonderful. They do. The life they have. A perfect life.

The woman, Sally, is pretty, like I might want to be when I'm her age. Which seems sort of older. And wise, was what Dahlia had said when we set their profile aside. Long ringlets of dirty-blond curls. The profiles: the photographs of them with all kinds of children, are they real? Nieces, nephews, friends' children. Their wedding in a backyard somewhere, super low-key. Will I even have one? I'm thinking. A huge Christmas tree in the middle of a huge city, everything lit up. And a letter to me. They all have a letter:

To a Special Person,

We want to thank you for your bravery and generosity in considering adoption. We hope our letter can offer some comfort. We think that your decision to bring a baby into the world is a wonderful gift, whether to our lives or another's. We hope we can give you some insight into our family while letting you know that, should we be lucky enough to have you choose us to love and care for your child, we will be committed to welcoming you into our lives as well, in whatever way makes you most comfortable. We are excited and grateful to be considered as the adoptive parents for your child; we would be thrilled to be the family to accompany you on this journey.

Sincerely,

Sally and Andrew

Who wants a letter like this? Let me tell you something: I never want a letter like this again. It says nothing. And everything.

Also I gather they have wanted a child for a very long time, too. Imagine wanting something for years and years. I can't imagine it right now. What I want and what they want has to be pretty different.

Anyway, she's pretty in a kind of hippie way. Long flowing print dress. Heavy brown boots up to the knee. The long hair and the bangs.

It's strange how I don't see the guys so much. I guess I'm more focused on the mothers, but when I make myself pay attention I see his hair is longish, all salt and pepper. Tall, slim. Jeans and a nice shirt but I can tell it's usually T-shirts and he's dressed up. For me. For me? They would have had good-looking kids, I can see that. I picture it. Their daughter. She might not look so different than mine.

Still, she is mine.

"Look," I say to Dahlia.

She looks out the window. Swallows. "Yeah," she says.

They walk up to the house and Dahlia sits on the couch and I drop the curtains, clear my throat, here we go.

"Hey!" Sally says, thrusting a small pretty bag toward me. I have learned already: the smaller the bag the better the gift. "Lotion," she says. "I hope you like lemon verbena."

Do I like lemon verbena? I really don't care but it's not something I have thought I needed.

I explain about Dahlia being there and they smile.

"That's nice you have friends who can support you," Sally says. "Is your mother here, too?" She looks heavenward, but I think she is actually looking toward upstairs.

"She had plans," I say.

"But she's supportive, too?" Sally asks. "About your adoption plan."

I nod peacefully. I am concealing the look that says, my mother is jump-starting this plan, lady. She is in front of it with a huge rope, dragging it, and we are hanging on by our fingernails.

I look at my brittle, bitten nails and then I look up and smile.

Andrew smiles back. "And the birth father is on board, too?" he asks.

Sally throws him a look. You can see those looks coming and going even when they're fast as a shot.

"Yup," I say. I can't get into it. Like, dude, talk to the agency, the lawyer, whatever it is. He's on board. He will sign her over.

It goes like this: What do you want, and what do *you* want? Who are you, and who are *you*? What do you want from the future, and what do *you* want? How are these the conversations?

Now Sally starts in about their summer plans, which involve being somewhere in the woods and painting and drawing. Getting out of the city, she says, like that's a thing.

It's all so cool but she interrupts a lot and he does this weird look-away thing and I can tell they might be over. Over like my parents, even though they still live together. Even over like Baylor and me but that is a different kind of over since it wasn't years together. It wasn't, like, a lifetime. I can see that but the love is still big love. Was. Rosaria rises up in my mind and I can see her long arms around him. Just loose and casual, like they belong there and it makes me crazy.

I am listening: we believe in public schools and museums or something like this and I am thinking of the other couples in the maybe pile: Orcas Island, the two guys from Oneonta, the baseball player and his wife. The vet and the real estate agent. Too many choices, really, but these ones feel like a leap of faith I do not have today.

"I love to bake," Sally says, and I can see Andrew make the smallest little laugh.

Is she a bad baker? Is she lying?

"What's it like to be a dancer?" I ask her. I don't think about it first, it just comes out. Because I really want to know.

She looks down and beneath her gauzy dress I can see her muscular thighs. "It was amazing," she says. "Dancing was everything to me."

I nod. "Was."

Sally's eyes are watery. "It's different now." She pushes her smile out, I can tell. "Not bad. Different. Dancing is for the young." She laughs and throws her head back, lionlike. Her long hair tumbles around her face. "It was a wonderful time. I danced all over the world. I have that with me forever," she says. "But it's over now. That part."

Andrew looks away and I can't tell if it's because he is letting her speak without getting in her way or if he just can't stand hearing this anymore.

"Now she teaches," he says. "She's such a great teacher. Her students are like her kids!" he says brightly. I can tell, when he pauses, that he's wondering if that last bit is a selling point or not.

For a moment, my heart, like, surges. With kindness for Sally. I like her so much. I can tell she's unhappy. This baby, it's for her, I know.

Andrew says, "Painting, though, you can do that forever." He grins slyly.

Sally: city, sweet, pretty, intense, a cool girl once, I can tell. But a mother? What makes a mother? I am wondering, hard. I want to know. If it's not the person who pushes it out, then what is it? Who I mean. Who is it?

"That's true," Sally says brightly, trying to save the conversation. "Being an artist, it's not for everyone." She looks at me. She looks so motherly and warm and desperate. Okay, I am thinking, she can do this.

But it seems wrong to me now and suddenly I can see the lights of the city fading out, fading fast. Andrew and Sally are disappearing into a crowd of people on a packed street. I can see her and see her and see her. Now she's gone.

I am a plane zooming over the building, three-dimensional in the night, I touch down, but now I pass it, through the clouds, back to the squares of farm land, the green grass, and cleared meadows. Back to the places I know.

I smile when we say good-bye. Sally touches my hair. Like just a chunk of it, which she sort of moves over a little bit.

"You are lovely," she says. She looks at me so intensely. "I hope we can talk again. I wish all the best things for you."

She is so *sad*.

I let them both hug me. I watch them walk out to that piece-of-crap duct-taped car. He puts his arm around her and she shakes him off.

I don't look at Dahlia and she doesn't look at me either. It's like we both know in our bones there is nothing to say. I go up to my room and Dahl follows behind and I see her pile of creek stones. She's built them like a stone wall around my little ceramic bowl of fake jewel rings I've been collecting out of the machine by the pizza place since I was a kid. I pick up a white stone, hold it in my palm, try to move on again.

IF ONLY

New York City

We come out of school and dang if I just don't want to hang in the park today, water fountain finally got turned on again, watch the freaks, listen to music, spring in the city, big grand arch beneath all that blue. Scaffolding is down! The girls with split ends and their acoustic guitars, flowing dresses, they tilt their heads together, open their mouths wide and go, *The answer, my friend, is blowing in the wind, the answer is blowing in the wind.*

Earnest as all get-out, I love it.

Two years and maybe I won't be here anymore. Maybe I'll go to some little college campus somewhere, a bubble crawling with ivy, where my father teaches maybe, but for now, I want to be right here on the ledge of this fountain, feet dangling in the water, here in the middle of everything.

Andre might bring his boom box. He's got one old-style, stuck with stickers, all . . . old. Turns it on: nineties hip-hop (East Coast, baby), grunge, bright bright pop, all kinds to bug the folk singers. Earnest as all get-out Where-Have-All-the-Flowers-Gone folk singers, I love them.

Me, I like the dog park. Teeny dog section separated so they don't get eaten by the bigs and means. Dogs are magic. Magic dogs. Ours has been dead just two years and even to say her name—Matilde—can make me cry. Dog sister. That is who she was.

Today is blue, blue sky, robin's egg or 9/11-style depending on your mood, right? Aight? I'll say 9/11. I'm in my striped cropped shirt, my high-waisted jeans, my flowered button-down, and I feel kind of blooming, like I'm all, I'm the girl of my own dreams.

Tina? Not so much. She's reading a cat vampire book and her black hair and black boots and she's perched on the back of the bench not talking so much.

Thinking also how I don't need to be in Brooklyn until six, when my mom gets back. She always wants to stop in and meet me at school downtown on the way home but today I can just be alone on the F and no one is going to murder me; it's not the eighties. I couldn't ride the train until I had to get to school. Great school. Education opens doors as my parents always say. (Picture the subway doors opening here.) But doors to what? She used to say, sell the silver, the paintings (Daddy's aren't worth much anyway), sell it all for your education. Give you everything. But then we got zoned for somewhere good. Or we stayed zoned for it.

This whole city. Best city in the world as all the good songs go.

So: Andre and Jonathan and Avi and me, all my boys, my gay boys (except Jonathan) and also my grump-ass Tina, it's all easy and lying around. And all I'm thinking is stupid jams like croquet makes me uncomfortable, how all summer my cousins and I played it at their visit house in Hudson, just stupid.

I say it out loud. "I hate croquet."

"I feel like that about Ping-Pong," Jonathan says.

"Random," says Avi.

"H'oh! Look at that cop. He's ticketing the piano guy!"

"No way," Andre says. He's got the box. "That is so rough; that is so un*just*. Ticketing an artist like that." He presses play on the old piece of crap: *Wreckin' shop when I drop these lyrics that'll make you call the cops,* goes LL.

Please shut up, Andre, I am thinking. I am sick of the artist rant. My father with the artist this, the artist that. I get it. He was an artist. His drawings are pretty amazing, though. When they got me he made me into everything. Drawings, silk screens, strange cubed paintings. It feels like he was waiting there with all his inks and charcoals and acrylics, just waiting for me to fill in this space he needed to make.

He makes art still. But mostly he teaches. Just north of the city.

For a while, it was the same song: Let's leave Brooklyn. Let's leave NY. Let's go where there's space for us to be. There's no artist class anymore. They said that until I was ten. Since I was three.

Then they got divorced.

They, like, missed the time to leave here.

I'm super glad. About the city. I am all in, city. I am all in, hang out with my friends in the best city in the world. I'm all in, look out across the water and see the buildings—morning, night, dawn, do you know how good the city looks, glittering, for always? Wherever I go next I am going to try to remember. How I used to live across from Oz.

Jonathan says, "I love my Ping-Pong table."

Freakin' Jonathan. Clueless Jonathan. No, take it back, won-the-jackpot Jonathan. Ping-Pong table in his Chelsea basement. Dad's in finance. Jackpot. Except his dad's in finance.

"Of course you do," I say.

"Best Bar Mitzvah prezzie I got."

Everyone looks at him and laughs, even Tina, because it's never not funny that Jonathan with his big huge Afro, his super-cool Africana shirts, all seventies-style, is Jewish. He's about seventeen feet taller than his super-tiny Jewish mother. That's why we're friends. Adopted, both of us. Me, at birth, Jonathan when he was one. Me, white as a daisy. Blue-gray eyes. I stripped my hair white blond—that went over well—but now it's dark as anything at the roots. What if I had ended up with them? With little teeny Ruth Seegar and cigar-chewing Dan Schwartz? Coulda been.

It's actually not that funny. Because I can go down a serious rabbit hole and wonder and wonder and wonder. If only. But what would I have wanted? To be, I mean. What?

Who.

I wanted my parents—these ones, the forever ones they're called and it's true, that is what they are, if only forever was real—I wanted them to stay together. I'm not going to lie. They divorced. I think they tried and tried and tried but sometimes, I think, you just can't in love. With adoption there's this extra weirdness, though. You can say it about most things in life, I imagine. Now I have a stepmother and a mother and a birth mother. But I just got one dad. Well, only one that anyone knows about. He's my only.

"Should we go play?" Avi asks.

"Not me, I'm staying outside," I say. Avi loves Chelsea. All the old guys, swinging sad, swinging happy. Moving. I feel like he looks around and it's, like, all the ways to be gay. Choose this or this or this. Or maybe he just is. I don't know. I'm afraid to ask.

I'm becoming confused over what a choice is anyway. Like can he just choose who he wants to be? Not choose to be gay or not to be, I'm not saying that, but choose how to do it. Like the way we choose how to be girls. Red lipstick, flowy printed skirt, cutoffs, fake eyelashes, leggings, shredded jeans, which is it? It can't be all of them, together, and you know what it means already.

Jonathan was chosen. (I don't mean because he's Jewish, by the way. . . .) I was chosen, too. And also not. Like the opposite of chosen. Ignored? No, it was of course much worse than that. Much darker. Have you ever known anyone who was pregnant and gave up her baby to be, like, in a *good* place? Like, a happy sweet place? No way, shit's sad. And all the forever parents who couldn't have their own babies. And me, opposite of chosen chosen.

She chose my parents. They were: cool-looking and creative and interesting and well educated and well traveled, and teachers and art makers and in New York and I think it kind of makes things genetically even because maybe that's what she wanted. From her own life. They were older, my parents. Forty-two when I got here. But did she know? How could she know? Like, maybe it wouldn't have been worse with her. Like, maybe she thought she was giving me the world but it wasn't that way. There is sadness everywhere. In everything.

But they named me Poppy. Just like a song. As for my name: A-plus.

The city seems to be the bargaining chip. For all of us. You leave it for this easy beautiful life. But you have to leave it. This. All these boys running through this fountain, shirts off, singing, droplets of water casting rainbows. These musicians, and also the food trucks and behind me this college, all different kinds of people, every color, wheelchairs, naked cowboys, good coffee, any kind of food you want, any price, American flags on little sticks, down the street Soho, over there the West Village, up there every museum you ever wanted to get inside of. My parents took me there. Every week. Jonathan got gold coins but I know who Kiki Smith is and I've met her, too.

My parents didn't make it through and my family keeps growing. Did she know? Would she have chosen them if she had known mostly it would be Mom and me and then Dad and me separate and equal as if it was a policy that came out of the civil rights movement. I used to wonder if that was allowed. If maybe I would get sent back. Be taken back.

By whom?

Lottery, luck o' the draw, but who's to say what's the luck? I've got cousins who had everything. Malibu dream. And they are sliding in and out of all kinds of misery.

Andre says, "Let's play some Baruch atah Adonai Eloheinu pong ball."

Jonathan fires him a look. The sun shoots through the ends of his hair. He looks like 1967. He goes to shul on Saturdays, even after his Bar Mitzvah. He's a social chameleon. But I know it costs him something. Has to, can't not.

Only in New York City, my grandmother sometimes says.

"D'oh!" Andre says. Hate it when they talk all *of the day.* Talking, I argue, is not a time stamp. "Some gefilte fish bagel table."

"Dude, that's racist," Avi says.

"And stupid," I say.

"Just so stupid," Tina says, tapping her boot on the bench. I have often wondered how many coats of paint are on these benches. Tina doesn't look up.

Everyone chooses to laugh at me. I can sometimes be more witty, when I'm trying. Or I could be serious, say: What are you afraid of? Don't hate. But I don't say this because I can't today. Can't be the voice of all the voices.

Don't know why but the day already feels ruined. Like clouds have passed *over* me. Being around Jonathan can trigger me like that. Makes me think too much about what makes me me. I'm telling you, it's not pretty in here always, not always my braided hair and aviators, not always so sunny and bottle blonde here.

My mom is a good cook. And my dad is a great painter. We all gave up everything for each other. My mom doesn't dance anymore. She's too old. My father teaches and has two young stepkids. He still has a studio but it's in a room in his house in Queens now. His wife's house. My dad just moved into it.

So I might not be here forever, I can't say. College. It could take me anywhere. What holds someone? What holds someone to where they're from, who they are? What makes me me?

New York.

New York City is my mother. All of them. And from them I have learned how easy to is to turn and walk away, to never look back, to never even say good-bye.

BRIDGET

"They don't have to be your friends. They are going to be parents. I mean, you know what I'm saying?" says Dahlia from across the table.

I rub my belly because I guess that's what we all do. Weather's bad so we're at our table at the café and I'm silent. I touch my belly, secretly, I don't even mean to do it anymore. When you see all the pregnant ladies on benches and walking through the mall do this it's because that's just what happens. It's like: to see if it's still there, to see if it's grown at all since last time you touched it, to see if it's kicking yet, to see if you are still the same.

Four and a half months and bigger and harder and harder to hide.

This morning my mom came and sat on the edge of my bed and said, "Bridget, this isn't something you can hide anymore."

Mama, I had wanted to say, just out of sleep, groggy, waking. But I got hold of me. "Mom." I shook myself awake. "Hiding is not the issue here."

She patted my thighs hard. "All children are blessings from God, and he has a plan for each one," she said. That, I know is from the Psalms.

"What is the plan, though?" I asked her. Because I'm open to God telling me what to do here, in a very specific way.

"You are also precious," my mother said. "To God," she said, and I felt the qualification, believe me.

Now, with Dahlia, who is just so much easier to decide with, I look down at you. But you are not the same of course, you'll never be the same, will you? Are you there in there? Who are you? I'm thinking about the night it happened. I want it to be clear: Baylor and I loved each other once. It was Sadie Hawkins and I wore a corsage and he had a boutonniere, a red rose. I bought it at the florist and I kept it in its little plastic pod in the fridge all day.

It was not the first time but it was nice, at Amelia's house, her parents were away. It was nice and it was slower than it had been the other times when it had been in, like, Bay's friend Eric's car, or the time in the yard, which is why I thought it would be okay, that once. Why didn't Baylor have a condom? I don't know, other than sometimes we felt bad about it—Baylor's mom is even more religious than mine; it's a born-again thing, I think. We always thought we weren't going to do it—that part anyway—again, but then we couldn't stop. Or we'd tease each other from across the room. We didn't want to stop. Once you've already done it why not always just do it? That will be the way it always ends now.

And now. Now. And.

"Yeah, I guess if I wanted the parents to be all down with the kids I might as well keep her. I want them to be parents, it's true, actual real parents," I say.

"What does that mean?" I can hear the hiss of the espresso machine. Like I need that kind of commentary.

"I think a real parent is an adult."

"We're adults," says Dahlia, but then she bursts out laughing. We were in love, though, is what I'm saying. Baylor and me. He was above me and we met up in all the right spots and it was hard to say no to each other because we didn't want to. Maybe she will know that one day: how hard it is to think ahead when right then feels just right.

"Do you think I should mention how much I wanted to be having sex with Baylor in the letters?" I pick up the pen to make a point of it, like I'm working, like I'm doing my homework here. "I want to let her know there was love there. In general, but also on that night. Like it came from . . . *good*," I say.

"Good sex? For reals? Would you want to know that?" Dahlia is talking with her hands again. Her nails today are purple and bright. They chip easily from all the ice-cream scooping. "I meant that your parents had hot sex the night they made you?"

"Gross." And it's this kind of talk that makes me realize that Dahlia got raised by Lulu, who never found religion like my mom. Or maybe she lost it? I don't know but I have always wondered how, two girls, same spot on the planet, boyfriends come from the same war, but everything is different.

Sometimes I can feel the girl parts of her, of my baby. Please don't ask me what those are. I mean, the body, yes, the body, hers. They are things you just know, like heart stuff, sparkly puffy sticker inside who you are things. Little girl things.

"You need new clothes," Dahlia says. "Let's go to the mall this weekend and just get you some stuff to get through summer."

By school, this will be gone. This could be gone.

Or could be with me.

"I can't." I shake my head. I mean, if I could just go to Eagle and pick out an array of shit in larger sizes, this wouldn't be happening, right? Or would it. Because even if I was a bazillionaire, I'd still be sixteen. "And I can't ask my parents for, umm, pregnancy clothes."

"Maternity."

"Maternity," I say.

"You can if you choose some parents," Dahlia says. "Let's choose us some parents and go to the mall," she says, and it's hard not to giggle.

I'll do this with Dahlia, not Baylor, I think. Not my mother. I look at her. It could be us who raises her, I think. Like some kind of movie about best friends. I look over at Dahlia. My beauty Dahlia, but why would she stay? It's a random dorky thought but it makes way more sense to me than my mother deciding she's going to get a rocker and start knitting little booties and help me do this thing, more sense than Baylor and trying to get him away from Rosaria. And relying on him. For anything.

"Let's do it," I say. Out the window the trees sway sort of violently. "It's going to storm," I say.

"Ooh, spring storm. Let's go out in it," says Dahlia.

I move to leave. Not many people know this about me but I am a girl who looks at trees. I love them. The shade the wind the green the swaying. Tree me.

I look up when we get outside and just start walking down to the creek over stones, careful not to fall though for a second I think I could fall and this would all be done with. I stop. I can't.

I look up and I can see my hopeful face over the tips of the leaves, this strange reflection that goes out into sky, like I'm dead or something. Here I am calling down from heaven, Dahl. Here I am hovering above you, above us. Why don't I know the answer, then? Why don't I know if; why don't I know who?

What I say is, "Thank you for helping me."

Crooked Dahl smile. And one foot pointed in the water. She looks up. "Of course. You okay?" she asks me.

I sit down, slowly, all of me now, bigger than ever. I imagine it. Walking out the door and all of this behind me, into the never was.

Dahl crouches next to me.

"I am." I can feel the damp of the ground spread along my growing butt. For a moment I feel like I've wet myself. Imagine one line instead of two. That is the smallest difference. It's everything.

"How about we raise her together?" I smile, cheeky.

"Sure thing," Dahlia says.

"Naah." I sit down, still my heart. "I mean, it would be nice, you know? Start like a new world. Made of girls." I feel around the soft mossy earth, soft as a baby's skull. What's under there? Is there a hole in the earth I can slip through, come out as the me before this happened?

Dahlia sits next to me. "Let's choose some awesome parents for the superhero you are housing in there."

I laugh but already my laugh is bitter, I can feel it. So many kinds of laughs, so many kinds of tears.

"I take it back," she says, rising to her feet. She reaches out, pulls me up. "You're the superhero."

"Yeah, right," I say. "If superheroes had premarital sex and got knocked up and can't figure out what to do with their lives."

"I'm sure at least one of them did," Dahlia says. "We see them all grown-up. In any case, they have now."

I can hear the steady rush of the water over stones. Clouds, flat and mean and gray, are gathering overhead. How many years have those stones been there? Smooth stones. Time. It all just undoes me now.

Dahlia is talking and talking. Girl superheroes. Baylor. Summertime. Fireflies. It's kind of closing in. I think of keeping her. Just for today I think it and I will not worry about anything else, I will just follow Dahlia home.

IF ONLY

Lansing, New York

Ideally the milk reaches a temp of at least 145 degrees, and not much higher because then it can burn. It's supposed to rest, just for a second or two. This allows the foam to rise to the top, which you need for layering. When you pour for a cappuccino, first fill the cup about one-third and then slowly add the espresso. Next, spoon some of the frothed milk onto the drink to fill up the rest of the cup. The espresso should be layered between the foam and the steamed milk. For a latte use a spoon to hold back the foam as you pour.

I learned this my first day of work, from my mom's best friend. She bought this café—the Blue Bird—a few years back and now she has a baby and so I'm working here after school to help out, but also to make some money other than from taking care of kids. Taking care of kids is exhausting. Coffee? A little less but I hadn't realized Dahlia would be so uptight about coffee—she went on to discuss integrating the flavors at length—but so it goes and so she is. Guess that's why she bought the café.

Anyway, I'm learning.

This place is outside of town—it hangs over a creek and there are evergreens surrounding it, which you can see through the big-paned windows. It's covered in ivy, which, Mom says, is how I got my name. You kind of feel like you're high up in the world. Or how I imagine it would be in the Pacific Northwest, at least from the movies I've seen. The café in town is where the college kids hang—here we get like true off-gridders who live way rural, or the hippies who come down from the monastery after a weekend of, like, not talking and eating mung beans. We also get regulars on their way to work, some professors who live out of town, near the falls. It's where my mom met her current and probably forever boyfriend, who teaches math at the less fancy college in town.

Now my mom walks through the door. That dumb bell that will drive me mad by 7:00 p.m. jingles, and she slides up, comes in all nonchalant like.

"Hey, Ivy," she says.

"Hey, Ma."

"Hmm." She puts a finger to the side of her nose as if to show me she is thinking, and hard. "I'll have a flat white."

"Sure thing."

"I was just in the nabe," she says, and if you can believe it, the word doesn't sound ridiculous on her.

Here's the thing about my mom. She's young. That's, like, her defining quality, always has been. Though I will say she is getting older now. Another thing: it was a nightmare growing up with her due to this. Well, let me rephrase. Not a nightmare, both of us were just kids. We grew up together. It was like having a sister except for when she tried to be a mother.

My mother was in high school when she had me. She didn't

finish; she got her GED later, and then she was in community college and she was always pushing herself to finish, and kind of blaming me for all her not finishing. My grandmother sort of raised us both, at the same time, which meant a lot of church and a lot of tuna casserole. Mom and I slept in the same room for the first ten years of my life.

It was confusing. But now? We moved out of my grandmother's house on Eagle Pass; we live with Mom's boyfriend now, near Ten Mile Creek. We have three dogs. And I'm about to have a sister. When my mother has her I will be the age she was when she had me.

Modern familying. That's what we do 'round here.

That my mother is a young mother actually gets more obvious as we get older. It's strange. Like, I thought we would be able to stop telling the story now, about how, yes, this is my mom, but she had me when she was sixteen. Now we look closer and closer in age. Like when we're old ladies? It's never going to make sense to some people. And I will say this: we have been on the street and had some men say some really tough crap to us. Like about how hot it is. Like, come here, ladies, twirl on this kind of crap. My mother goes deep ballistic then. That is when she is mama bear and I am baby bear.

I like being baby bear, I'm not going to lie, because there were a lot of times in my life where I was comforting my mother when, looking back, I could have used some of that love for myself. Some of that mama-ing. I don't get to be the baby bear very often.

I look at her growin' belly now as I warm the milk. I decide

I'll warm the cup because, well, she is my mother and she did raise me. Sorta.

"Caffeine?" I ask her.

She shakes her head. "De," she says, and I know.

She's due in two months. I wonder if she'll marry Joshua. He's older—forty-five. Divorced but no kids. Such a nice guy but let me tell you there has been a trail of assholes behind us. The trail of tears, as they say. A whole country wide. And also I wonder what it means for me. Will I be like some weird aunt to this kid? I already told Mom I'm not going to be their live-in babysitter. It feels to me like she thinks we have some kind of exchange going: She gave me her teen years and now I have to give them back and over to this baby.

I just don't know if I'll mind yet. How do you prepare for a baby? I wonder if my mother knew. I think she does now, judging from the amount of baby stuff that has been accumulating at Joshua's house.

I get to the right temp, and after that second of rest Dahlia insists on, I pour the milk, lifting the pitcher high the way she showed me. Then I push the cup and saucer toward my mother. I look up. Her face. I have been looking at this face for so long I can't even see it anymore. It's just my face with someone else's skull inside it. But I'm sixteen and I'm not my mother and I have no plans to be staying too long.

She doesn't seem to realize that I'll be leaving soon. Mom will have her baby and maybe she and Joshua will get married and maybe not and she and Dahlia will hang out when their kids play together and they'll talk about what all the moms talk about, which, far as I can tell, is eating and shitting and sleeping and how much wine they need to drink to get through it.

"Thanks, babe," Mom says as I push the warm cup and saucer toward her. I can see a chip on the saucer but I don't say anything. Dahl would call it homey.

I watch her take a sip. "Hmmm," she says, smiling. "Delicious."

I won't be stopped by time either, you know. It's not like they keep going and I just sit here, waiting.

"Very professional," Mom says.

"Thank you," I tell her.

But one day I'll be done here.

One day I'll be gone.

IVY

2017

The sun is just about down over the ridge now and the tree line looks to be on fire. It's beautiful here. In all the seasons. All the times of day. The explosion of light. I got that fire on the inside here right now.

Mo puts her hand on my shoulder. "You okay, my banana?" That is what she calls me, still, sometimes. "I'm sorry. We weren't keeping it from you really. Just waiting for the right time to give it to you. This is a hard thing to read."

The letter had been opened. And not by me. And sent five years ago. I am still wrapping my head around that. Mo and Mom talk honesty and integrity and their truth and all of it and here I am with this bulky opened envelope.

I look up and they're here: my people. My family.

My mom is reaching for my hand. "No more secrets," she says.

I nod, but I am trying to understand. I turn the envelope over: no return address.

I put it aside on the table. This is a moment and I don't want to give my parents the pleasure. I just don't want them to see me read it. Like, what will my face look like? It feels private. I want to be on my bed, I want my journal, juju charms, I want to be alone. Or no, I want to be away from my parents.

Dinner finishes fast. Claire's mom picks her up and off she goes and my parents don't make me do anything to clean up. That's how bad they feel, and I don't mind saying, I take advantage. I leave the dogs downstairs and I stomp around, then go upstairs without telling my moms I'm leaving. Is that a three-girl thing? The third girl always tells the other two where she's headed.

Not tonight. In my room, alone, but I'm no good at being alone. I hate it, really. Does a tree make a noise of no one hears it fall? It's that kind of thing.

For reading the letter I text Patrick. I open my jewelry box—that ballerina, jerkily turning, still—and I put on my silver locket, feel the heart, cold against my collarbone.

Hey, GG, I write, which is short for Gummy Goo, which is what I call him for some dumb reason that has to do with an infantile gummy bear in a soaped-up bathtub video we once saw.

G here, he writes me. *At my post. Just left practice.*

"Practice" is in Alex's garage, because it's heated and his parents are divorced and he lives with his dad. I've watched. Alex with this epically large mouth wide open, his huge white teeth almost swallowing the mic, and Jonny, the skinny wild-eyed drummer, and Mikey, the sweet guitar player who holds hands all day long with his girlfriend, Kristin, a cheerleader. There's also Megs, a quiet boy with a shaved head and acne who came from a private school in Idaho—maybe rehab—who, as far as I can tell, just appreciates the music and, like, carries the equipment around. Sometimes there are girls with them, thrift-shop girls like Sophia Mallack, black straight bangs, tasteful emerald nose ring, any kind of baby doll dress, lace-up Docs. Or Audrey Siegel, with one side of her head shaved, her rolled-up T-shirts, her ripped-up jeans.

Alex is the one you watched. If you were watching the Farewells, you don't really notice Patrick at all.

But I do. I like the one who's not in charge.

TT? I write. Talk Talk? Is it strange to have a different language for everyone? Like my thread with Mo and my thread with Mom. Those are different. I speak all different people. Shame I'm so crappy at real languages. Why is that? Because they're like math is why. No one ever tells you that but learning languages is nothing like what I love to do.

K.

The phone rings: Don't laugh but I like it poppy. Jem, *This time, baby, I'll be bulletproof,* that's my Patrick ring today. Bang, bang. His pic comes up, swoooop. Brown hair, dimple on the chin, sexy sideways crooked grin. Hey there, Patrick. Hihihi.

"There's a new letter." I don't say hi, how many ways do I need to announce myself anyway, and I want to keep calm. I want to read Patrick the letter.

"What letter? Hi."

"Yeah, hi hi hi. Birth mom letter. My moms have been holding on to it. Like, keeping it from me, actually."

"Wow, not what I was expecting."

"What were you expecting?" I'm moving around the crime scene that is my room, then sitting down at my computer and trying not to go online when I'm talking to Patrick. We promise each other no S and M, social media, while speaking but both of us do it anyway. I'm handling this pretty stone. It's cold and hot. I am trying to *focus*.

Okay. "Something to do with me? Like the letter you've been writing to me that is telling me all the deep dark things you never say to me."

I giggle. "What would that be?"

"Razzer."

"Am not. I don't even want to know what you were thinking," I say. I don't actually. It will be soon, the what he wants to know. It will be soon that I will tell him when. I just have to be sure.

"Read it, Boo." It is our dumb solution to "Bae," which I hate because it's not a solution at all. Even my mothers use it. They think they can say anything because they're lesbians and that somehow makes them cool for eternity, but it doesn't. At all. I can't follow Mom on Instasham for this reason. Mo isn't on and doesn't know much about what's happening and Mom posts pictures of all Mo's flowers and plants, also her own special ancient grain breads. You look at her feed and it's like a *National Geographic* page.

But let's face it, Boo isn't original or great either. It's awful.

Anyway. I'd say come over and I'll read it in the real but

Patrick lives ten miles away and that's over twenty-five minutes on these roads. (No as the crow flies out here in the woods says Mo. I know: it took me years to really picture it. Crows flying.) It's over twenty minutes to get anywhere. Alex's garage is forty minutes from me, which is why I rarely go there. Oh, and that's without the snow.

Shaking, I take it out. Nice thick paper. Watermarked. "Can you believe my parents had it?"

"Really?"

"Yes. I am extremely pissed off."

"That's so unlike them, don't you think? Did they give you a reason?" That Patrick is parented by hippies can be slightly annoying at times, most particularly when I am looking for outrage. It's like they patchoulied it out of him.

"I don't really know."

"Well, just read it," Patrick says. I picture him on his little twin bed, the brown sheets tightly tucked in. I picture him turning all his records over. His *vinyl*, another term I don't especially go in for. It's just a record. That's what it was always called, why do we start calling it vinyl now? There is also probably sage burning in his hallway.

I clear my throat.

"Okay, but I just need to say the handwriting is really lovely, also big and really careful."

"Neat."

"Okay."

I begin to read.

July 23, 2012

Dear You,

You're nearly twelve now. Ivy. I know it and I can feel it. I feel you every day. It's something I can't explain. I feel the day you were born, the way it was when you came into this world, and I feel you growing, too. Who are you? What do you love? That's what I don't know.

I can't lie to you. I have struggled. But I have worked to make my struggles meaningful and now I'm set free. I walk for you and I walk for me and I walk for the future us. I see blessings everywhere. In the natural world. Here, among the trees, along the water, wherever I am traveling, I celebrate you. Every day. What could have broken me didn't break me. I don't know you but I know you and you have blessed my life. Your moms, too. It's the happiest sad really to know that you are there and happy and healthy and cared for, the bitterest sweet. That out of the wrong came this perfect right, came you.

Do you think about me? Do you look in the mirror and wonder? I am sorry for that. I had planned to be there, always. A child can never have too much love, I know that, but I had to slip away. I hope you can feel me the way I feel you. I wonder what I am missing. Braiding your hair. Reading you books. All kinds of dresses. All the things mothers should do. You are the light inside me and I hope you know I am inside you. My light.

I was afraid of becoming an adult for so long but I am here now. In the world of the grown-ups and I am okay in here. I know I missed your childhood.

I walk for you I walk for me I walk for all the people in the world who need my blessings. My struggle has been meaningful. I am not scared anymore.

You, my darling, are the light. Never forget that. If only I had known that everything happens for the best. So that's why I want to tell you: Don't look for me. Be free.

There is purpose. To all things. If only I had known it.

Love,

Your first mom

I feel numb when I stop reading the letter to Patrick. I'm gripping the stone, tightly. I sort of wish I hadn't read it out loud. I wish I could stand to be alone. It feels awful to hear her voice come out of my mouth when I can't hear her.

I stop for a moment. Stand still. Look up. Hold out my stone. But I don't feel the light. I can't see a thing.

There's silence on the end of the line. Who's going to break the silence? I decide it is for once not going to be me.

Only Patrick can be quiet and okay with it a lot longer than I can.

"What?" I finally say.

"Wow."

"Wow?"

"She's so smart. She sounds like you."

I gasp because it literally takes my breath away. She sounds like me? All this time I thought all I'd ever gotten from her was her shaggy brows, her eyes maybe. But I got other things. Deep-down-under-the-earth kinds of things.

"Like a hippied-out version of you. She could be making hemp clothes with my mother at the farmers' market this weekend, you know? And play the tambourine."

"Funny, Patrick."

"Sorry."

"You think that sounded smart?" I ask.

"I do," Patrick says. "Like smart about the world."

I nod but he can't see me. I place the letter aside. I place the stone next to it. I look at them both as if they are some kind of still life Claire might want to draw.

"Sad, though. What happened to her? You met her, right?" Patrick says.

As if he doesn't know this. That first year, she was around here, and then she was gone. I wonder I wonder I wonder. "Yes, but I don't remember it at all. I was a teeny baby. I've seen pictures that make me think I remember but I know I don't." It's all frozen, these memories. But then again, all our memories are frozen, aren't they? I can't make my memory *move*. It's only pictures, always. Just photographs. "I just remember the pictures."

"Sad," he says.

"I want to find her. At least I think I do."

"Are you sure, B?" Boo Bae Busy Bee.

I'm silent. For real now, not just for effect. Then I say, "I do. I think I do. You know, I'm sixteen."

"You know I was there for the birthday party, right? That was me, like, with the bass? Looking and sounding amazing. We sounded rad."

"You guys kind of sucked." I laugh. They really did suck. I

think they had played three times before that night and maybe once since. Not sure when they'll be playing again for a crowd other than in Alex's garage.

"We are good! You never know, you know. Basil Henderson's band got a contract remember. I mean, it's not all stupid."

Basil Henderson's band, *Guesswhat Ross*, from our town, got a contract *in 2001*! They are legend here. They went out to Los Angeles and became hard-core and then kind of disappeared. His mother is still in the English Department at Cornell and every two years or so some student makes the connection and that's kind of the end of that legend.

"Sorry," I say. "Not stupid at all."

"I know," says Patrick. "We suck." I can practically feel him brush the shock of hair out of his face. "Sixteen, though. You always said when you're sixteen . . ."

He could be talking about my birth mom or sex and I don't want to know which he means right now. "Yes, G, when I'm sixteen there's a whole year of it. Anyway, she was my age. What if that were me?"

"A baby?"

"What, you can talk about, umm, doing it with me, but you can't talk about what happens a lot of times when people do it?"

"Ouch," Patrick says. "Too hot." He makes some annoying sizzling sound.

What's he doing in his room? I hear the quick tap tap of his computer, which drives me bananas. I can tell he's trying to hide it. "I hear you," I say.

Now there is the sound of what I think is a pencil knocking

on wood. His headboard or his desk. Which is it. It's a huge difference. One is not paying attention and one is all ears.

"Let's go find her, then," he says.

I'm silent now because maybe this is about to be a ton of complicated feelings. "I don't know," I say. "I mean, I talked about it
with Claire today, too."

"Oh."

"Don't say 'oh.' She's my best friend."

"And me? I'm what?"

"My fave boy."

"Boy? Man!"

"Anyway," I dodge, "judging from this new letter that's been
in hiding for nearly five years, she doesn't want to be found."

"You don't know that. You have no idea what's happened to
her in five years."

My breath stops. "What do you mean?" Because I have of
course thought of the option that maybe the window has passed.
Like she said. She missed me and I missed her. Maybe she is
gone. From everywhere. Five years is kind of a forever.

"I don't know," Patrick says. "A lot can go down in five years."

"Mom and Mo, they might have more info, you know? An
email or something. That's what Claire thinks anyway," I say.
"But maybe this wasn't all of it. I mean, maybe there's more stuff
they're hiding from me."

"Hm-hmm," he says. It's because of Claire. He wants it to be
only him, but there is always also her.

You know what Patrick did once? He got a doctor to take an
X-ray of his chest and he gave it to me. My heart, he'd said, And

there it was, the outline of it. The ribs were ghost white against the black X-ray, blocking the heart, and the arms were off the page but they were outstretched, too, like he was reaching out to me. I'm giving it to you, he'd said. This cliff-jumping, bass playing boy, handed me his heart.

Later I found out he had asthma and compromised airways, and so he had to get a chest X-ray every other year anyway, but still. He gave it to me. His heart. In the cage of his bones.

I love him. If the heart was in color? It would be gold. It would be painted golden. I'm sure of it.

"They have her old address, I know that. Where they visited her, like, when she was pregnant. With me. I know they met her before."

I imagine her in a doorway somewhere, leaning in, kind of coolly waiting for my arrival. Like an old movie or a bad commercial for cheesy perfume or laundry detergent or some feminine hygiene product that should have been discontinued long, long ago. I know she's thirty-two now, though. She not sixteen. She's twice my age exactly. Or: I am half of hers. Half of her. But my features and that quilt, that dumb dollhouse, empty inside but for the furniture my parents filled it with, that's all she ever gave me, that I can see. Smartness? It comes from everywhere.

Is it a house? That door, I mean. Is it to a house? Is it empty or full? Is it clean or dirty? What did she become?

"You think she's still there?" Patrick says. "I mean, fifteen years."

Who is inside? Her house. "She says she's been, umm, walking. Walking where? Maybe she's still there." I hold the letter up to the light the same way I held that X-ray. The paper is uneven in spots, less transparent in some places. There's a watermark of what I think is a globe in the center. A sphere. I want it to mean something but I think it's just fancy paper. "Maybe," I say again, cradling the phone.

"Thank you for reading that," Patrick says. "I feel like I know you better. I just want to know everything."

If he were next to me, I'd be supposed to kiss him, but part of me still wants to roll my eyes. Why? Why can't I be serious and all in? What do I know about Patrick? The band. Loves dogs and bikes. House smells like musk and used books.

I lay the stone in the palm of my hand. I expect it to be cold but it is strangely warm.

"Patrick!" I say. So suddenly. It's strange. Can you be erased? Like, what if the butterflies don't flap their wings at all? What if they never get out of those cocoons to begin with?

"Ivy!" says Patrick. "What up? What what."

"I'm just sort of overwhelmed by everything I guess."

"I get it. I'm thinking what it would be like, like, to have this one thing you don't know."

"Sorta. I mean, that leads to lots of other things. It's not just one thing. That's like the cherry on the sundae, but there is all the other sundae stuff."

I hear him laughing. "So much sundae stuff. Making me hangry."

"Can't believe my moms kept that letter from me. I mean, why would they do that?"

"Well, yeah, that's upsetting you, it is. I can tell. They love you, doe. You know it. They must have had their reasons."

"But other things upset me. Wars. Killing bunnies. They don't keep me from looking at news, really." They kind of do, though. And I can't look on those pet rescue sites anymore either, which I used to do all the time.

Patrick is silent. "I think what's really bad is how sad she is. How she disappeared and then this came out of nowhere. Like out of air. That's . . . weird."

It is. *I have struggled*. That word. What does it mean? Really mean? I walk for you. *Now I'm set free.*

But what does she look like? What would it be to see her face. Is it my face?

My room, red, red walls, dragonfly lights tracing the doorframe. The warm rock in my palm.

Where is she now?

BRIDGET

June 2000

"Yes, this is she," I laugh nervously. "Me here," I laugh again.

I'm in my bedroom. The clock says 4:00; they're exactly on time. And Dahlia is across from me, just off work, cross-legged, piling up creek stones and then knocking them down. I love the sound of them. Like teeny bowling balls hitting teeny pins.

"We're on a conference line," she—Ruth—says brightly. "Dan's at his office. Aren't you, honey?"

"That's right!" He practically screams this. Then I hear a kind of muffled sound like he's covering the phone and talking to someone else.

"Dan?" says Ruth.

"Sorry, sorry, lots going on here. Busy, busy!"

Does Ruth sigh? Maybe.

"Hi, Bridget," she says. "Thanks so much for talking to us. We are grateful to meet you over the phone and we hope we can meet you in person, too!" She seems sweet.

I nod, then realize they can't see me. I cradle the phone and walk over to Dahlia. Pick up a stone. "Yes," I say. "Very nice to meet you. Phone meet you." It's just so awkward. I look over at my wall of movie posters. Baylor's sister, Mandy, works at the movie house and she used to give me the ones she didn't want. I love them. *Virgin Suicides, Holy Smoke, American Beauty.* "Really nice," I say because it hits me that I need them, too, now. I am selling myself so they will want me. But I need them to be good. And then I won't have to get a job.

"Do you have any questions for us, honey? What for instance did you like about our profile?"

I hear more muffled talk on Dan's end of the line.

"Dan!" Ruth bites into the conversation. "Dan!"

"Yup! Here I am. Ten-four!"

"Maybe it's best if Bridget and I speak alone first."

I'm not sure who she is talking to, me or her husband. The smooth stone. I place it at my cheek and it is warm from my hand.

"That's okay," I say. "We can be quick and decide if we want to meet. I chose you because you have so much to offer a child. That I guess I can't." I'm quiet now. My fear of adulthood has turned into an ache I cannot name. I sneak a look at Dahlia across from me on the bed. She's rolling her eyes already, which is not helping.

"We sure can," says Dan. "We want to spoil our child rotten."

I clear my throat.

"Oh, honey, don't worry," Ruth is laughing. "'Spoiled rotten' is just Dan's way of saying we do intend to give the child whatever he or she needs. We can do that. If we are lucky enough to match with you, if you choose us, we also want to be sure the adoption is as open as you like."

I look around. Still there's Dahlia on the bed. The digital

alarm clock hasn't moved a minute.

I swallow. "Open? Yes, open."

"If you want to see the baby, get pictures and letters. From what I've read, open adoption, where the adoptee can be in touch with the birth mom or get letters and pictures, that's what's best for the child. And for the birth mother of course. So important."

"Yes, open," I say. These terms again. "I don't know yet," I say. The counselor also said, you will just know when you find the right family. Trust me, she said. Every situation is different.

Last week, when Dahlia and I had looked at Dan and Ruth, I admit I liked all the stuff. The apartment in the sky. And the stuff meant that they could send me money and I could put this whole job thing out of my mind. The pics in Times Square and at the opera, the two of them digging into huge bloody steaks, *the* big city, really, a place I have never been to. Their city feels different than Andrew and Sally's.

It's just a few hours from where we live and I have never even been there. Why? I wonder for a moment if I can get a free trip out of this. What if this baby, my baby, could go there and live there and be a fancy person with a playroom and a thousand toys and, I don't know, like a piano, or a pony or whatever. Taxicabs. *The Nutcracker.* I can't give her any of that, but the secret here is, suddenly I can. Suddenly, I can give you the world.

The world without me in it.

You.

"Open."

Power.

"Listen, I'm going to sign off," Dan says. "Talk to Ruth. She can tell you everything about us! Okay?"

"Yes," I say.

"Bye, honey," says Dan, and I have this feeling he doesn't remember my name.

"Bridget," I say, but he's already gone.

"Of course," Ruth says. "We are here to help you now. Tell me," Ruth says, "what do you need?"

What do I need? Hmm. The list is long. Or very, very short. I don't know how to answer her but I tell her I'm good and healthy, like I'm a dog and I've got all my shots, and my parents are supportive and the boy knows and will sign the papers, sign our baby away, and my friends are helping me and I just want some time.

"I'm glad you've got support. Time," Ruth laughs, "is the one thing we don't got." But I know she is serious. "How are you doing in school?"

I start to tell her. About English class a little maybe, reading *Ordinary People*, or how I hate chem, just can't wrap my brain around it, but then it hits me. She is asking for the baby. Like how will the baby be at school. Will the baby be smart or dumb? "Good," I say. "Hard to concentrate right now but good."

"Of course," she says. "It must be, my God, how could it not be?" she says, and I flinch.

Before I hang up I ask her: why. "Why are you adopting?"

There is silence. "The truth is," she says. "I have tried and tried and I can't have my own children. Biological ones, I mean. I have done everything. The science, the herbs, the acupuncture, the diets. I have done IVF seven times."

I don't tell her I don't know what IVF is.

"But I was traveling so much and Dan is never home, so." She stops herself. "He will of course be home for a baby. We both will be. Obviously. He wants a child as badly as I do, he just works very hard."

I can hear her swallow.

"We want to be parents," she says. "More than anything." There is a pause. "I want to be a mother. And I'll be honest. It will be easier to be the mother of a white baby. It just will be. For all of us."

I shut my eyes. Well, at least she's said it.

"There aren't that many white babies," she says when I don't speak.

Why does this make me about to cry?

"I'm sorry for what you've been through," I say. It's what I am going to say to all of them I decide. I'm not going to talk to Ruth and Dan again, though. I know this more than I know anything. They are wrong. For me. They might be right for someone else or maybe they will figure out how to be right for the next one. The next white girl they talk to. Or maybe they'll figure out how to make one from their own blood.

"You too, Bridget," Ruth says, and I can tell she also knows that we won't be talking again.

I've got what all of them want. This baby inside me, she could inherit the world, all sky and moon and sun and stars. All for her, this world. It's already getting away from me. I don't know what I want in it for me. How am I supposed to know all this now? The future the future. It is as far away as the planets. But I feel it growing nearer. I am scared of it.

"Next up," says Dahlia because she can read my mind. Or maybe I'm reading hers now.

I look at her. They were wrong. Stuff is only things. I wish I had them. She knew all along. What does she think? Who will it be?

IF ONLY

Wyoming

"I guess," I say, patting the neck of my horse. How original, I'd thought when the stable person brought her over to me, but I've gotten attached in these past few hours. The thick ropy muscles of her strong neck. The deep, glossy brown mane, shiny enough to make me want to ask her about her shampoo. "It's okay." I look out. The mountains are slammed against a blue sky. Pasted upon it. At Starlet's hooves and spread out before us on the endless meadow we just trotted across, Indian paintbrush, glacier lilies, and larkspur bloom. That's what our guide just told us grew here. I'm listening.

"For chrissakes, Jaz. It's a million-dollar view is what it is," says my father. "You are too spoiled," he says, but he's smiling. That's been his mission. It's all he knows how to do. I can tell he's dying for his cigar. Gloria, who runs this ranch, shook her head and took it away from him, literally slipped it out of his mouth, as he got up on his workhorse. I watched the woman helping the other guest squint at him in disbelief. Streaked hair. Blue eyes. Feather earrings, long as her shoulders. He started to put up a fight but I mean, come on, a cigar on a horse? And Gloria doesn't seem like a person you argue with. "A million bucks," he says to Gloria, winking, and she touches her hat.

The helper? She leapt up to help.

Money money money. Even in the metaphors. My mother would have lasted about five minutes on this trail. She's back at the ranch getting a massage. She'll be reading on the back porch, her short gray hair wet from the shower drying—and frizzing— in the evening sun.

Tetons mean teats. That's what Jonathan told me last night, our third night. We've got two more nights here.

"Jasmine," he had said, and I had stopped him right there. "Jaz," I said. "I hate Jasmine. It's just not me at all," I had said. "I mean, it's a Disney princess. I still don't know if my parents knew that."

Jonathan had scoffed. "I think they did," he'd said. "I think Ruth and Dan sure did."

"And Jonathan comes from what, then?" I'd asked, looking at him sideways.

"No idea."

I know who he thinks I am. I know what everyone thinks.

"Titties," he'd said, laughing, and it kind of thrilled me, felt it in my belly. I thought he would reach out and touch me right there and maybe I'd let him, why the hell not, I'm on vaca- tion. From school, which is far away from home. I'm all New England–style now, look at my boots and pearls and, yup, my riding lessons. Hi. You're not going to be wrong when you think you know me. Mostly.

I'll let him tonight that's for sure because he's different and weird and lives here at the ranch with our guide right there, just the two of them. I wonder about families all the time. Like, why adopt me and then send me away to boarding school? What's the point of it? Am I for later when they're all old and tired and needy? I wonder about that. I shiver now thinking about what I'm going to let Jonathan do to me tonight after everyone's asleep and the pretend bonfire on this pretend ranch has gone to embers. There are hammocks and pillows and all kinds of rolling hills. There are so many places here. To do a million things.

"What if you were me and I was you?" I had said last night.

"Seriously? If I were white? I don't think so," he'd said.

"You are the only black person here," I had said.

"Do you think I didn't notice? Thanks for the memo."

I hadn't said anything.

"I'm good," he'd said. "I'm all right. I know who I am. I'm good out here. It's summertime now and all kinds of people move through here. Being the only black guy has its perks." He'd raised his eyebrows, smirking. "And everyone knows me. It's small-town life. I like it."

"Do you know your mom?"

"Do I know my mom? You know my mom. She made you your dinner tonight. She's taking your cigar-chomping father riding tomorrow. Do not go there. You don't know anything about it. Have a little respect." Jonathan had gotten up, probably to trek on out.

"I know something about it."

He'd paused.

"I'm adopted," I had said. It's no big deal but the sentence hangs between us. We are so different but he can't deny in this we are just the same. Lost or found, which was it? Which was it, Jonathan? Ha, I tricked you, you thought you knew me exactly. So tell me: lost or found. Wanted or unwanted. Where do you weigh in, Jonathan, who thinks he knows what's inside me, all of it, my everything.

Another raised eyebrow. His hands had cupped his scalp, hair shaved close. "Yeah?" he'd said. "So do you know your people?"

"My people? You mean my cigar-chomping father?" Because really, guy, it can go both ways. "He's my person."

He'd nodded.

"No," I had said. "One day maybe I'll get a name or a number. If I want it. Maybe."

"I know my first mom. She named me."

"I never heard that," I had said. "I use birth mom."

"Well, I was with her for a year. I call her my first mom. Just always have. I know her. Not the guy. It was, well, anyway, I know her. More like, I knew her."

I had sighed deeply, inadvertently. "Oh no."

He'd nodded slowly, moved in. The kiss is like nobody's business, I swear.

"First time you ever kissed a guest, I see," I had said, laughing.

"First and last," he had said, and that kiss was like, I can't even say, like, *deep*. Big. But short. Nothing to lose style.

"I see her," he'd told me. "Even now." He'd shaken his head. "Can't really talk about it. It's not a great sitch but it's mine. That's all I want to offer."

I look over at his mom now. Gloria. I don't know, kind of everything normal about her. Tomboy-like. Levis. Tank tops, thick gloves, toothpick in her teeth. So good with animals. Sweet inside, you can just tell. Hard outside because who knows what happened. She doesn't like me but she's not seeing everything. I'm used to that, believe me. It's not the first time I've been judged for my long straight hair, my clothes, my white teeth. It's my armor. My outside. It's my superpower.

"Night," he had said, rising. I had been surprised but I know how to play. Not my first time at this kind of rodeo either.

"How much these beauts go for anyway?" my father is asking Gloria now, and for a moment I think he's talking about the mountains. Honestly, it wouldn't surprise me. You can put a price on anything, can't you? I heard my father once, putting money on trading the weather. My parents have gotten everything they've ever wanted because they can buy it. Hi. I wonder how much I cost them.

But he's talking about the horses. "Dad," I say. "I think this is the most beautiful view I've ever seen." I mean it. From up here, it's like there's clarity. I've been on a mountain looking out. I've been there in summer and winter. I've skied and hiked all over Europe. Been on mountains, but never really looked out at a mountain from this distance. The titties. They're astounding. Why can't I just say so. "Thank you for bringing me here."

Starlet stomps. My father turns to face me. He's old now. He has always been old but now I really see it. Lines like the crevasses in the mountains, all filled with snow. All that smoke. All those late nights and God knows what they do there. All those men. He's in a world of men. He won't be around forever.

"My Jaz," he says, soft as he goes.

But already I am heading back down the hill. I feel Starlet move beneath me, the stomp of her hooves in the soft earth. She is slow going down. She is careful. Behind me the mountains soar into the sky.

IVY

2017

We've taken a lot of our *Crossroads* submissions for the cover of the last issue of the year to Claire's house tonight. It's not my job to find the one but I like to look anyway. I like to be *involved*. More like controlling, says Vanessa, our managing editor. I've never heard anyone disagree.

Claire is a few blocks from school and I like walking home with her. That feeling of living so close, not needing a bus or a car to pick me up and put me there. Everyone gathering themselves up, taking their time at their lockers, wanting to get out but not being forced. Then the walk down the path, through the old alley. It's like a secret we all know.

Downstairs is their regular family doing all their regular family stuff like homework and television and video gaming and I really do think there is a meat loaf in the oven and maybe mashed potatoes happening on the stove.

This is why she keeps me around, I think, Claire. To cut the regular.

Today I'm on my belly, feet in the air, and I'm just thumbing through some of Claire's photo books for ideas.

"I know we're supposed to use student work, but don't you

think this pic of these twins would be awesome?"

Claire pads over from where she's sitting at her desk and looks over me.

"Freaky," she says.

"It's either this or this photo of ripples in a puddle strewn with leaves. Called *Reflection*." I hold up a grayish photo with just that.

She makes the universal symbol of gagging, which has always made me feel like gagging myself. "There's some good stuff, don't you think? Somewhere?" Claire keeps thumbing through the images.

"Doesn't have to be a photo, does it?"

Claire sits on the bed and starts paging through the books. "Something weird," she says. "Edgy. Like, look at this." She holds up another shot of two old ladies having lunch or tea or something together. I instantly love them.

"Is that edgy?" I ask. "Or just old-fashioned?"

"Look at the lipstick," Claire says. "Edgy."

I sit up. So fast I'm dizzy for a second. She has a sloping attic ceiling up here and I practically knock my own head off. Claire is staring at me, full on. "What?" I ask her.

"Let me draw you," she says.

I shrug. "Sure thing. You've drawn me before. It's not such a big deal."

"I know," she says, getting up and going to her desk drawer, taking out her many nubs of charcoal and her artist pad. The big one. "I just feel like this will be a good time. You seem sort of you today. Very Ivy."

I don't ask her what that means. I'm not sure I want to know. Instead, I sit and she cocks her head this way and that. Holds up the pad, sketches. Looks at me, looks at the pad, looks back. It's really like a parody of someone drawing someone but I try not to laugh and I don't say anything about it.

I can hear Dominick, her brother, playing video games downstairs, screaming at the screen, or himself, who is to say. No idea what game he's into. I'm not allowed to play video games. I mean, at home. Which means I don't play them out because I suck. So that's a thing that just completely got away from me. That's another thing Patrick and I have in common. He wasn't allowed to have a phone until freshman year. We are both video clueless.

Claire draws. "Stay still!" she says.

I have my shoes on her bed, which would drive Mom insane, but she doesn't seem to care. I futz with my laces, look out toward the window. I sigh. I brush dog hair off my jeans. I sigh again. I hadn't realized how much I sighed. Do I do that in general? Or just when I'm trying to be still?

What is it, twenty minutes of sitting?

Something like this.

"Okay," she says, erasing, using the side if her hand to brush off that rubber eraser dust. There is a final cock of the head. Final look and then look again. I can see her writing now. And then Claire turns the pad around to face me.

It's shocking, really, though I can't say why. It's not perfect or anything. I'm cross-legged, as I am now, *criss-cross applesauce*, and I'm looking down at my Converse. But I'm also sort of looking out at the same time. You can see three-quarters of my face. My hair is pulled back like it is now, and there is a lot of hair escaping, frizzing out, really, though it looks cool and spiderwebby in the drawing. My fingers are pulling absentmindedly at the laces of my shoes.

Ivy, Searching it says in cursive beneath it.

I look up at my friend. She wears one of those adultlike apologetic smiles. She's on her knees and her hands are in her lap. "You," Claire says.

I look back at the drawing. It feels so strange to be looking at yourself. Is that me? Not exactly, I don't think, but she's got something in there that feels precisely right. My eyes, I think.

Or something inside. Something you can't see.

I look like her, in that photo. Just after I was born. The side of my face. The slant of the nose. The eyelashes even. They belong to her.

I touch my cheek.

You know how when you look long enough in the mirror you become a stranger? Like, you're not you anymore. You look for yourself, but you're just not there. It's like you're lost to yourself the more you look for you.

But when you let your best friend draw you?

Then, you become exactly yourself. You become absolutely who you are.

You are found.

BRIDGET

June 2000

I wish I could take away that night. The night we said, oh, screw it, ha-ha, I get it, it felt so good. So, so good. But gosh, if I could take it away and just be hanging out with Dahlia deciding what we were wearing out tonight and who would be there and if it would be a bonfire or the broken-down house in the woods or maybe someone's parents would be gone again.

It's only afternoon anyway. Summer days are not the same anymore, that's for sure.

"Let's take a break, go to the reservoir," Dahlia says.

I imagine it. The tiny shore we'd sit on in our bathing suits last summer, pretending it was by the ocean. Even white white me had a good enough tan that summer. Now I shrug.

I would give myself over forever to have what I'm doing tonight be what I was deciding right now. To be leaning into the mirror to put on my lip gloss and throwing myself a kiss before I turned to walk away.

Things I do need to decide: get a summer job that does not involve a bathing suit or seeing anyone I know, clothes that will fit, parents for my baby. That's it! This is what I'm thinking when we get down to the reservoir and who do you think I see there splayed out on the rocks in her red bikini, smooth as a cat, but Rosaria? Baylor's next to her, smoking a blunt. I can see them from above. Like bird's-eye view, and I grab Dahlia's sleeve. She shakes me off and scrambles down our usual way but, hello, I've got this extra weight and in that weight is a baby and I have to be careful now. Or not, I think for a horrible second. I could fling myself off this giant rock and be done with it, with her, but who knows what would actually happen? Then or later. There is always a punishment, seems to me. I will never go unscathed.

I used to be so good on these rocks, scramble, slide, climb, sit here and watch the days go by, all the ages I ever was here, growing up, watching my life go and go.

"Hey-ho, look who's here," I say loudly to Dahlia.

Baylor sees me and pretends it's no big deal, but I could mess some shit up for him and fast if he doesn't pay some attention. To me. You pay attention to me, boy, you understand me, I want to say, which is something I have never thought to say to a boy, not ever.

Rosaria, man, she is so gorgeous, she slides up to sitting. No flab. I don't know how her smooth stomach can make room for her to sit. There's nothing there. And when your skin is that golden you can't see anything but shine and glow. I hate my pasty white skin right now, the cellulite forming all over me in little cottage cheese chunks. And big ones. I am a mess. I know I would never look like Rosaria, but in a perfect world I could look, I don't know, like I'm from Paris or something. Like white cool, skinny, good, interesting clothes. I know my hair looks crappy, too. Rosaria's is long and black and shining. What is she even doing with Baylor Atkins?

"Hey, Bridge. Hey, Dahlia," he says, calm like Baylor always, always is. It's a guy's way, isn't it? No high-anxiety pyrotechnics. Not unless there is another guy there. Then it's all brother shit and crazy hugs and handshakes, almost like they want to touch each other as bad as they want to touch us.

Wanted to.

"Don't hi me," I say.

He rolls his eyes.

"How are you?" Rosaria says. "How are you feeling?"

"Like you give a shit," I say.

"I do," she says. "I give a shit. How are you feeling. I mean you don't have to be a bitch to me about it but I do feel bad for you."

Dahlia puts a hand on my shoulder because she knows that will set me off.

"Don't need your pity," I say. "So do not."

Rosaria nods. "Heard."

"Baylor, I'll tell you later about shit, but you've got to ask, like there is some serious shit going down here." My voice wobbles. It always does now.

"I know," he says, all contrite.

Yeah, right. "So why don't you call me and ask me?"

Baylor stands. "Because all you do is yell at me."

"When have I yelled at you? You came to meet those people once and that was it. That's bullshit. I don't yell at you," I yell.

JENNIFER GILMORE

There, I can hear it, okay I get it. But it's not like I don't have a reason.

"Exactly," Baylor says. "Meeting those people? Those freaks? No one asked me anything. I just sat there like a freakin' moron."

"Well," I said, raising eyebrows.

"You know that kid is my kid, too."

Baylor points to my stomach and I resist covering it up, to shield her or me, I can't tell.

"What you are doing with it matters to me."

"Me too," whispers Rosaria.

"The baby is not an it."

Dahlia says, "She. She's a she."

I can tell it hits Baylor, stomach-style, winded I mean.

"My cousin has one, you know," says Rosaria. "A girl."

Baylor is nodding. What is this one his, too? But really, I had no idea. "Pam?" I ask.

"Hmm. No way my grandmother was going to let that kid be taken away from us."

I felt that. Pow. Serves me right I guess. She has to see it on my face.

"I didn't mean it like that," she says. She's putting on her T-shirt now. Covering up. Covering over. I want to hate this girl but I can't.

I feel the sun. I love the sun. I think of last summer here and of Nelson at camp, the two of us in that big chair. "Got it." I turn to leave.

Rosaria stands up. "I didn't mean it," she says, coming closer.

IF ONLY   119

"Like that, okay? It probably would have been better if she had. I mean, her life is ruined."

Baylor watches her. I wonder if they're doing it. I wonder, what with her cousin and that baby and what with Baylor and his, this, well I wonder if anyone will ever learn. Or at least be safe about it.

I nod. "Okay."

"I didn't know when we started," Rosaria says, pointing at Bayl. She slips on her jean shorts. Actually, she has little-girl legs. The shorts are all frayed and perfect and faded like they've been drying in the sun, but she has those stick legs shooting out of them. She is young, I realize now. And me, I am getting older.

"I didn't either." He flicks his blunt glumly and it skids onto another rock.

Dahlia says, "Well, we all know now, don't we?"

Rosaria goes to hug me. Her skin feels so warm, from the sun and the warm rock she's been lying on. And summer. And Baylor's love, too. That is probably part of it. And I can feel her big boobs and her small waist and she can probably feel my belly that's growing by the second.

She drops her hand on my rounded stomach. She grabs Baylor and makes him touch it, too. He resists at first and then he gives in, lets his hands cup my belly. The three of us are all looking at each other. Dahlia also reaches up. And right then, I swear to you, she kicks. For the first time. I feel it and I look at them.

"Did you feel that?" Baylor asks, astonished.

I smile. "That was the first time," I say. "I swear."

They all scream and jump back and Baylor goes, "D'oh," in his idiotic way.

Then all the hands are gone.

Then it's just me. I place both hands on the sides of my belly. Like I said. Then it's just me.

IF ONLY

Lansing, New York

I'm twirling and twirling and then I fall down. Look up, there's my father, spinning, looking down on me.

I giggle and giggle, like I'm little again, and when I realize it, I straighten up. I smile. I smooth out my dress. My dad, all trim now that he's lost a bunch of weight. It feels different to dance with him. I miss the belly, I think. It's the way I always saw him but now all the women here look him up and down.

"Hey, papi, you looking fine now Rosaria get you to the Weight Watchers?" they ask him.

He pats his belly and roars.

Rosaria comes up and takes him by the hand. They're still in love, I can see it. My father would follow my stepmother to the end of the world. Once she tried to leave him and he slept on her mother's doorstep. She stepped over him on her way to work in the morning. Another night he held up an old-school boom box and played Alicia Keys below her window until a neighbor came out in her pj's and curlers and smashed it to the ground.

Those are the stories anyway. Rosaria still sings that song, all the time, while she's cleaning or in the shower. *Some people want diamond rings, some just want everything, but everything means nothing if I ain't got you.*

The story of their love is always the story of her leaving and him doing something goofy to get her back.

Like losing all that weight I guess.

My stepcousin comes up, all dressed up in her quinceañera dress, like the top of a really tacky cake, like a model in a store I'll never shop in. *Oh you know, that tonight I'm loving you*, goes the music. You gotta have one, Rosaria always teases me. That's how you become a woman, she says, pinching my cheeks, God's blessings, she says. I feel bad because Rosaria and my dad just have a son together, my brother, Frank, who is eight, and I'm pretty much her only chance for a party like this, but it's not right for me. I love Rosaria and I speak almost perfect Spanish now, and she is like a mother to me, but I can't do what doesn't feel right. I guess I get that from my mother.

Wherever she may be.

Tonight I want all of you tonight. Give me everything tonight, the music says and here comes my grandfather to take me by the hand. He twirls me around, but that's not really how you dance to Pitbull. "You gotta eat, little girl," he says.

The food has been amazing, it's true, but all that meat makes me feel tired, and I guess he can tell it ain't happening because he dances away, over to his niece Pam, and her daughter, Georgia, who's a few years older than I am. We used to do everything together until she got to high school. Now she can't be bothered with me and I don't really care because she is the one draped over the steps in C building, where all the fuckups hang. She's not going anywhere pretty, I know that, but tonight she looks so sweet with her hair all curled around her face, a flowered dress cinched at her tiny waist. The Vasquezes are gorgeous. They make dumb decisions, but they are drop-dead beautiful.

Outside the window are trees. The lake. You can see to Aurora this winter.

Dad pulls me up. "Let's dance, whitey," he says. He's a face sweater and that's happening to him now, which I try to ignore. *Tonight*, it goes, bass shaking me to my bones. I like my dad in the wintertime, when he comes in from the tree farm he runs, smelling like the cold and the pine needles and that smell of when it's just about to snow. I like winter dad best. All flannelled and gloved and hatted and far away.

But I let him hold on to me and pretend to lead me with his little shuffle. All the guys here are awesome dancers and this, along with something about the way he always feels so left behind, makes it seem like my dad is older than other men his age. He just seems so out of step with it all. I guess we both do.

Or maybe it's just out of step with this. I lift my head up from his chest. The big banquet hall. The salsa, the disco ball turning and turning. All these platters of cabrito and barbacoa getting cold and congealing with fat. It's all celebration here but that's not the kind of people he comes from. He comes from angry people. My grandmother sits out front of her crappy house and yells at all the people who cross her lawn. She's never given me a present. Ever.

I got lucky, I know, and so did he. We both know it, too.

Rosaria comes over and pulls me off him. I think she's going to take him in her arms, but instead it's me she takes. Like when

I was little, being held by Rosaria, looking down, her beautiful black hair that smells like all kinds of flowers. Only I'm bigger than she is now.

She pulls me away and under the spinning ball and she twirls me and twirls me and twirls me around.

"Ahhh," I scream, looking up like I'm catching snowflakes.

"I love you, my daughter," she says. "God's blessings. Quinceañera or not, you are my only one."

IVY

Don't know how, but today after our weekly *Crossroads* meeting—
we voted two poems ("This is Why I'm Crying" and "You are
the Sun, the Moon, and my Stars" by a sophomore lacrosse
player I didn't even know could spell and Alex's poem, "Punk
can save your soul and other daydreams") as well as a short story
by a Dungeons & Dragons–playing senior about a girl who turns
into a mermaid to go looking for her grandmother's jewels that
were lost in a shipwreck—we end up in Alex's basement.

He was hanging around outside the office, waiting to see if
his poem got voted in after the meeting.

"You're in," Claire said, and I hit her. For one, the poetry is
my beat, and for another, we are really supposed to notify our
writers more officially, by email.

She shrugged. "I love the line 'Nothing feels good but remembering and singing to you.'"

Alex grinned.

Is that a good line? Maybe. I like the feelings it gives me.

"Song lyrics," he said as we were headed into the hallway.

"How cool," Claire said. "I'd love to hear them sometime."

He nodded, but this is the thing with Alex. He doesn't care.

He got what he wanted. The poem in the magazine. Looked at us long enough to make sure that happened and now? Nothing most likely.

"You guys can come to practice if you want."

Really, I thought. Wow, thanks so much, Alex.

But Claire said, "Cool. We'll come then," without even checking in with me.

That is the other thing Claire likes about me now: Patrick.

Alex looked at Claire, and after following Alex as he jumped on and off his skateboard, here we are.

"Hey!" Patrick says, confused. "I didn't know you were coming out here."

"Alex," I say, as if that is an explanation. It kind of is, though. Everyone wants to be around Alex. He's like this bursting star or something, all jaw and muscles, and he's an artist like on this cellular level. He writes, he draws, he makes music. He grows stuff. He's like an art *brute*. What makes me choose the person who isn't in charge?

Wanting to be wanted I guess.

"You could have texted," says Patrick, and he's right, but what exactly would he be doing differently if I had?

Mikey's girlfriend, Kristin, has cheerleading practice, so it's just us groupies today.

Soon as Alex steps up to the mic and, after checking the set list that they've pinned to a cork board behind the drums, truly, a *set* list, they launch into: *Down in Joe's garage, we didn't have no dope or LSD, but a coupla quartsa beer* and sure enough they hold up forties.

I almost never dance, unless it's with Mo's brother, my uncle Larry, who tends to drag me around at his kids' Bar Mitzvahs to pop tunes like "Can't Stop the Feeling!" but sure of herself fully formed Claire bops around to this Zappa stuff, slow as the beat. She watches for Alex, closely, while he pretty much eats the mic, but his eyes are cast downward, always.

That's when I go sit down.

"We are," Alex says very solemnly into the mic when the song is done, for this crucial audience of two, "the Farewells." And then the drummer, gets a beat, too slow. And then? *I—I—I—I—I'm not your stepping stone.*

Alex still doesn't look at Claire, or any of us, and I see it register with her, how he's just *performing.* And then, after three songs, practice is over, like the set list says, and Patrick and Alex and Mikey and Jonny all congratulate each other on their most excellent playing and throw out some places they might be able to play soon. Everyone is like, yeah, totally, in *town,* and I feel Patrick come up beside me and take my hand. *She's with me,* it feels like he's saying. It's nice to be claimed—chosen—and all but it's also something else I can't name right now.

"I assume I'm giving you a ride?" Patrick asks me, his face super close to mine. Hot breath on your neck in a cold basement, by the way, feels both wonderful and disgusting, should you ever need to know this.

I nod. "Obviously," I say. I imagine waiting here for Mo to come for me, just with Alex and Mikey, and a wash of gratitude sweeps over me. "Thanks."

Darkness creeps in through the little basement windows above our heads. Daylight savings—we live for it—is a few weeks away, and Alex's yard, and the stones and bushes along the path to his front door, are fading fast into the night.

Claire lives close by. Everyone lives close by compared to me, but I tell her we're going, to see if she wants to come with.

"I'm good," she says, putting on her cute wool beanie. Claire being cute and also timeless. Claire being Claire.

"You're not going to stay, are you?" I ask her. Because I don't want her to go all puppy dog over Alex. I don't want her to be like everyone else; I want her to stay Claire, fully formed, not like everyone else. Powerful. Don't go regular, I want to tell her.

She shakes her head. "No, I'll walk."

I breathe out. "You okay?" I check in. Take the emotional temp.

She nods.

I shrug. Everyone starts pulling on coats and scarves. It's cold up here forever it seems. When we're all ready to go, Alex trots up to us.

"You guys leaving?" he asks, surprised like. "So soon?"

Guys, man. Guys.

But Claire is strong, she's *back*, and she says, yeah, she's got stuff to do at home, and we all trundle out into the dark blue evening together.

The stars are coming on, they're coming up. I look up before getting into Patrick's Subaru. It's clear tonight and by the time I'm home the sky is going to be filled up with them.

I want to say, let's cut his stupid poem! But that's unethical. Or, should we come to practice again another time, I want to ask her, or something like this, but I don't know what her deal is with Alex and I'm not going to find out here. "Bye, honey," is what I do say, pulling her hair back and hugging her.

"Bye!" she says, dodging all my intensity—what else is new?—and I watch her start to jog out of the drive and down the street.

I get in the car. Patrick turns on the heat and cranks the music but I turn it off before I even recognize it. "I had enough for the day," I say. I turn and look out the window, wave to everyone, as Patrick backs out of Alex's driveway.

Patrick's hand on the stick shift. Reverse, first, second, third, now I put my hand on his. The road is empty but for a truck I see far up ahead with its blinker on. The road bends and curves, the head lights flashing on trees and mailboxes, all the barns so close to the road. Patrick's hand is warm and when he turns it over after shifting to grab mine, it's a little clammy. I hear the swish of his parka as he moves his other hand to wipe his hair out of his face.

It's about a half hour home. I think about Mom pulling a bubbling lasagna and one of her breads out of the oven, maybe a ciabatta, soft and doughy and dusted with flour. I picture the light on when we pull up. The smell of the house, when I walk in, like yeast and honey and oregano.

I look over at Patrick. I sit back.

I'm almost there.

BRIDGET

July 2000

What if it was only the me part I was figuring out. Just like everyone else. I will be this or that. I will be better now because I know I almost couldn't have been. That thing I should be.

But I waited too long. Who knew how many ways there were to cry and this feels like all the ways at once. I had thought I would just find the right place to raise her and I had thought that would bring me some kind of peace. Doneness. Dahlia brings out some more profiles. They're all to a special person. And what makes me special? Us special. The special people are all of us. All of us with the babies we don't want. Or can't want. And can't keep.

We are the birth mothers. That is who we are. The special ones.

I'm heaving and Dahlia comes over to me. "It's going to be okay." She takes me in her arms and she feels so, I don't know, *bready*. I feel like I am being surrounded by soft warm bread.

My mother knocks at the door. "Bridge?" she says softly.

I'm quiet.

"Can I help you guys?" she asks.

"I'm okay, Mom," I say, and I can hear her hesitate and then move away from the door. Now I hear my mother on the stairs. This gets harder the more she grows. Just saying. The more I feel Dahlia hugging me the more I feel the baby, too, her, and it's harder and harder. "Why can't we raise her together. You and me! Let's do that. Us."

Dahlia laughs and it looks a little like that Andrew's city laugh, which is not a real one. So many ways to cry, so many ways to laugh. Remember when it was no or yes? Happy or sad? *If you're happy and you know it* . . . clap. That's all it used to be. *Clap clap.* Stamp your feet. Happiness.

Now she's flopped on my bed, feet in the air. Her feet knock together.

"You have to do this soon, Bridge," she says. "I mean, damn, she's kicking."

We are pretend girls, I sometimes think. We are doing the things that make us seem like girls. Look at our fingernails, our hair. Is that what makes us girls? Or is it this thing growing inside me? This girl thing? Is that I made a baby what makes me a girl? What will make her one? What kind of a girl will she be?

"Like there is a deadline here. And the sooner you know the sooner you can relax and keep to the plan and not be so worried all the time."

She's right, but what if I don't want a plan? The longer I don't plan the more of what happens will just happen and I won't have to decide a thing.

If she's been here, growing, right here in this house, my mother's not exactly going to throw her out the window.

"Also? She wants this. She will want this. It will be right, I promise," says Dahlia.

"I do the pros and cons a lot," I say because it's true. "But all the pros for keeping her, well, those are mostly pro for me." I get quiet then. It's sad but everything good about keeping my baby has to do with what will be good for me. What will be good for her? To have everything I can't give her. There are some pros in there for me: following my dreams. But I don't know what those are anymore. I never knew them, not ever. I am not one of those girls.

Dahlia nods seriously. "You are the mother, though," she says. "Don't forget that. That is important."

"Let's keep looking." I throw the pile of portfolios the agency sent on the bed. They shimmy and slide across the duvet, fan out. All the desperate people who want babies. All the people who can afford them, can afford all the lawyers and agencies it takes to get one. It's sad, really. Why? Like, what makes these people want to pay someone to help them pay someone to help them pay someone to get a baby. How do they know what they want?

I know that's not what it is. When I dig deep and see what I know is that these people deserve to be parents and they can't be and they too have left their lives at the altar and they too are waiting to be heard. For someone to hear them.

Is that person me?

Dahlia sorts through their portfolios like we're playing old maid or something. She holds up one with a question on her face.

"They look like all the others," I say. I don't know how you decide.

"Here!" Dahlia says. She tilts her head, touches the puppy they're holding close.

I look over and I smile. But it is not a questioning smile. It's true, they are different. One of the parents looks just like Dahlia's mom. I touch her face in the photo. "She looks so much like Lulu." And then I say, "But really? Two girls?" Because I have been taught what I have been taught about people and what the Lord will and will not accept. It's hard to shake all that but I will say this: it's a lot easier now that I don't get woken up for church anymore.

"Women," Dahlia says. "And yes," she says, quieter, almost, I don't know, devout. "It's them. I can tell."

I have been taught so many things. Good real things and also things that might not be true. I am learning to see that I can be faithful and I can question. I get it. I do. It all makes sense.

"Just look," she says. "Closer. In a way, it's like us raising her. Like you wanted."

I look at Dahlia. Her face is so close. She runs her fingers over the faces in the pictures, tilts her head. She looks like Dahlia, too—the eyes and the sweet mouth.

"Just look," she says.

Carefully, I lift the portfolio out of her hands.

"They look great," I say.

Now Dahlia is the one crying. "I love them," she says.

BRIDGET

July 2000

I want answers. For sure ones. Ones that say: yes, do this this way. There is no other way to do it. The reason people go to church I guess but I don't go anymore. Like this? No way. My mother doesn't even shake me awake to come with her anymore.

I go back down to the creek, alone. What would it be like to just know what will happen? Who we'll all be? I have just been and done and acted and here I am. I have never controlled what I have been thrown toward.

Summer is all around me now. And down here as I wobble down to the grass I can see it still, people hanging out, the blunt roaches, crushed Pabsts, the cigarettes, sometimes a smashed pipe, everyone but me living like a kid in my town lives. There is the crash of sticks breaking and I know it's people partying out in the woods. I know these woods and all the secrets we get to keep in them. I know everything now but it's all behind me.

I untie my Docs and stumble along the little mossy bank, set my feet in the cold water. I feel the swollenness contract, and I wait for it, to go wherever the creek is going to take me while those boys whoop and hurl themselves off the cliff rocks down where the creek opens up. It's far away and close at the same time. It's just me, waiting. Just me and this baby kicking inside me. What does she want in there? What if I could know what she wanted? What if I could know who she wanted?

She wants me. Now she does, but after? She won't want me. Anymore. Who could?

When she grows up? What will she be looking at then? Just me.

I look out. I crouch, feel my long skirt along the water and then run my fingers through the water, too. But all I have is my awake dreams, which are more like small wishes: how I wish my mother would crawl into bed with me and hold me like when I was a little girl, scared of the dark, scared of everything, scared of my father. And I'm thinking of what it would be like to be with Baylor again, before this, like when I made a winter picnic with a thermos of hot chocolate, and it was just nice sitting out here and talking. I remember the air so cold we could see our breath. Our breath, clouded up and knocking into each other. I'm thinking of raising this child, one last time let me think it, but it can't be with Baylor and it can't be with my mom and I'm thinking Dahlia would be the only one. I imagine us, older, I don't know, like twenty-five, walking down the road, this beautiful nine-year-old swinging between us.

What do nine-year-olds do?

I'm thinking of those women.

I trudge out of the water. Feel the grass between my toes, wait for my feet to dry. They're already swelling up again when I go to put on my boots. I look at the creek. I look at the creek running over those rocks like they have been doing since the beginning.

Maybe I know. Maybe now I just have to trust myself.

Two mothers. Three, if you count me.

That night after dinner I go back up to my room. Just me. I read the profile again. Their letter to me, which is really a letter to anyone like me, says, "to our future best friend," but it actually feels like they mean it. Can you tell the real from the fake? Only when there is the real. Maybe. I feel myself calm. I look at their lives. Flowers and good food and foreign cities and beaches and so many people smiling. I move to the phone. I dial. It rings and rings but no one answers. I imagine the phone in the room in the house in the neighborhood in the town in the state in the country in the world. It is all just my imagination.

I smile. There's this feeling you get when you know: calm. That part is true. She already feels like family. I've never had it before. For the first time in forever, I breathe. I mean, really breathe.

I put down the phone.

But I know I'll keep calling. I'll keep calling and calling until someone there answers the phone.

BRIDGET

These are the things that happen. I choose the parents. And they choose me. And then it's summer and I lie around the house and my mother yells at me for never going outside and never getting a job. She sure didn't like who I chose, but she was so happy to have a for-certain plan, she didn't fight me. Also, the parents help with the rent and they buy me clothes and my mother is into that. They come for a visit and we go on a walk to the creek and we talk about the future. Their future, really. They ask about mine, but I don't have any answers yet.

I don't go back to school. I can't. I'm so big and uncomfortable and worried and I just want to stay inside and watch television. They send me all kinds of books. I read some of them. My mother goes to school and gets my homework and I try and keep up that way. I plan to go back. I have to go back. This is one of the reasons, right? So that my life can go on. I can be all the things I'm supposed to be.

But what are those things?

They do not send me a juicer, but I try to take good care and eat better than just the French fries and pizzas and potato chips I crave. My mother makes me eggs in the morning. With avocado and tomatoes on the side. I feel like there is something about that I will remember. I don't want to remember the rest, though, like watching kids walk by on their way to school, that September smell. Leaves turning. People pulling their outside furniture inside. That smell. I get why people used to go to the nuns. Go far away and come back all new. Empty and new and ready now for a brand-new start. A whole new season.

The parents—hers—make it easier because there is a plan. Now I can just get through these days and stick to the plan and then it will be over.

It happens when I'm alone. I've crossed the creek and gone into the woods and I see something awful there: a fallen nest and a pile of feathers, some bloodied. I can't see a bird body and I don't know much about birds, but I know those are not the kind of feathers that have molted. They've been ripped out. Or something. But the bird, she's nowhere to be found. I feel what I guess I would call horror. Like, what will I do now? I start to sort of kick at the overgrowth of dried leaves. It's autumn now full on up here and the leaves on the trees are on fire and the dry dead ones on the ground are piling up and up. But no bird. No mama.

There is a feather. Separate. Longish. Shot with blue and white strips. I lean down to pick it up. It's perfect. I hold it up to the light, look at the trees between each little line of silklike feather. It's like a kaleidoscope of sun and bark and changing leaves. I'm dizzy from it.

That's when I go to the nest. I lean down, afraid to touch it because of that thing where the mom animal will never come for anything that has been touched by a human. Is that true? I don't know what's what anymore and I certainly don't today, but it scares me into not wanting to interfere here. And then I see what's next to it: the nest is empty but for one perfect blue egg. This, I only now realize, is why they call it robin's-egg blue. It is that blue. There has never been any other shade like that color.

I lean down, look around, as if I'm about to do something horrible, but really it's to see if there are birds watching. How crazy is that. Birds watching. The nest looks not so much like a gathering of sticks, but like it's been spun with them. Like there has been some kind of sorcery, some swirling of the forest to make this nest for this single perfect egg.

But now, closer, I can see there were other eggs. They are smashed and cracked, there along with the leaves and the bird's feathers. Something horrible has happened here. Still, though, the perfect blue egg. All alone.

And that's when I feel it: this sort of pop and then this fluid down my legs. I realize it's on: I scramble up and over the creek, back up to my house, calling for my mother. She comes running out of the house, wiping her palms on her jeans, car keys in her hand.

And then: it is five hours and two big pushes. It is the most painful thing I've ever experienced, even with the medicine I had to beg for. It is the most important moment of my life. It is the worst thing that has ever happened to me. It is the feeling of what it's like to break my own heart. It is the way she slides out. It is the slippery animal seal of her, it is her there, the most beautiful perfect being. It is me thinking, you are going home but not with me. It is me thinking, I have loved you first, I am the first person to ever love you. It is me thinking, please. It is Daisy, Rose, Maple, Ivy, Marigold, all the things that grow and grow and grow, you are perfect. It is the way I can't smell you enough or look into your blue eyes for too long, touch your perfect fingers and toes. It is how I don't want this kind of love to ever leave me, but I don't see how I can survive it. It is meeting you today.

It is the parents and it is me seeing them and knowing that she is theirs now and that is how it has been written, but it is also knowing that I worked so hard and did this, did this, and housed her and all of it and it was for them and not for me. It was for her, I know, but it is me not being able to feel that right now. It is me being split and sewn back up again, but inside, it is empty. It is the nurses saying I shouldn't hold her for the night but it is me doing it anyway. And it is me not looking at the new family, her family, the family she belongs to, I know that, but it is me not being able to see that right now because she is mine and she is me and I need her. It is me breaking in two again and again and again.

I can tell they're terrified. I can see they don't want to push me, that they know she is mine until she becomes theirs. They hold her like she's made of glass. They give her back to me too quickly, hot potato, and smile, and one of them, the one who looks so much like Dahlia's mother, is weeping. She leaves, weeping. I can hear her in the hallway and I imagine her back against the wall, body-shaking movie kind of weeping, the kind I've been doing for months now. It's going to be one of us now. But which one? Maybe it doesn't have to be me with my back up against the wall. Not today.

They are gone. My mother packs my suitcase, folding all my underwear and T-shirts, carefully, as if they are baby clothes. So carefully. She waits and waits but she is gone, too.

Come, I text Dahlia. I think, we will deal with this later, how uneven our friendship has been. I will be good, later, but now, please, help me.

And here she is. Dahlia in the doorway, her head a mass of curls, her strong arms outstretched, each hand touching a side of the doorframe. But she doesn't come inside.

"Help me."

Behind her is a line of people all making their way in: Baylor. And then I see my mother again and Baylor's mother and Rosaria. They are all in a line and they come in. I hide my face. I want them all gone. I want it to be only her and me now. That is it. Everyone else is somebody else that is in the way of us. But they move in around my bed. They circle and close in. I feel like it's a vigil for me. Like, where is the minister with my last rites? What is happening? Then I think:

Maybe I'm already dead.

They hold hands, the string of people who know me. Their heads are all bowed. Maybe I have already died.

"Please give our Bridget the strength to know what this little baby needs," says my mother.

I want to be angry but I also want that strength. I want the strength to break my own heart.

She is in my arms, my flower, my garden. My mother is reaching for her.

No! I am screaming No no no no no no. It's all the times I have ever wanted to say it. Everyone looks terrified. No no no no. To all of you.

She is crying too now.

My mom comes next to my bed, kneels down. Please don't tell me she will be praying. I cannot have the praying here. "We're here for you," she says. "To help you."

"Tell them, Dahlia," I say to my friend. "I need time. Tell them!"

My mother wipes the hair out of my face, the way she did when I was a toddler. I remember it just when she does it, but it's like I've always held the memory with me.

"It's going to be okay." My mother stands and nods toward Baylor and Rosaria and Dahlia and Bay's mom.

No one looks at me as they walk out the door.

My mother holds my hand but I nudge her away. I look over at the empty doorway. I look down at this little baby, a loaf of bread in my arms.

"I'm okay," I say. "Mom. I'm okay. I just need some time." I am willing myself calm. But all it is is this crazed panic inside.

"I'll wait outside in the hallway," she says.

Dahlia kisses my forehead. "Right outside that door."

I watch them leave. When the door closes, I look at the dark corners. It's okay, I say to my baby. To my daughter. That's when I whisper to her what I'm going to do.

IF ONLY

Montana

Ziiip. Her face is covered in black hair, shaggy, no haircut in, what, years, it seems. I still trim her bangs. Crooked.

"Hey," she says.

I lean back into my book. I shrug.

She climbs out of the tent and comes over to the little table we've got set up here. I have no freaking idea where we are. Somewhere cold and blue and lonely.

She shoves her hands into the pocket of her hoody, tucks her hair into the hood. She looks like a superhero or a criminal. Rubs her hands together like there's a fire she's warming over but there's no fire here.

"What's for breakfast, Ivy?"

I don't look up, slide over some cereal bars we picked up at a Target—where, in the last town? Bozeman. Butte? I don't know and I don't really care either.

"Lovely," says my mother. She looks over at the green Coleman stove on the table. Cold. We got cereal bars but we did not get Sterno. Don't ask.

I glance over at her. Watch her open the wrapper with her teeth and then look up. She smiles at the sky or the tips of the trees. They're turning now. Either way, whatever she's looking at, it will be cold as all get-out soon.

"I'm thinking we'll go back to the ranch. What do you think? You can go to school again."

I ignore her. We spent last winter there and I went to school and it sucked. The school sucked and being new and a sophomore sucked and it was both too big and too small for me. I was all caged up and also it was like I was all free, too. You know? I mean it could have been that if I had friends. But the ranch is a good place. Huge. Our own room. People cooking for us. Jonathan. He is the one thing about going back but he won't care anymore. He might be gone by now anyway. Nothing is permanent on the ranch.

My book: *Black Beauty*. It's my TV, internet. It's all I get out here, really. I love horses.

Mom looks at me. "Hello?" She flips her hair out of her face, her shock of blue.

I look at her. "Hello." Like a dare.

"Remind me how we got here again?" She kicks at some fallen leaves. She uncovers a bunch of feathers. A huge pile. She kneels down.

Does she mean, like, the hitchhiking? With the professor, the mother of twelve, the truck driver? No one was safe. Did you know that? No one. Or does she mean it, like, not in a physical way, like how did we get here, on this earth, in this forest, doing time in this tent night after night? I used to love it. The sleeping bags zipping together, a gift from Gloria, who runs the ranch we'd been working at each summer. Now just the sound of it—*ziip*—makes me want to flee.

I get up. "I'm going for a walk," I say.

"Be careful," she says.

I just start walking. The trail out from the site leads to a small rise, and I can make out the mountains. What are they? Gallatins or Crazy? I don't know. I think they're the Crazy Mountains. Or I like to think it anyway. I wonder what's over them. Like, what there is for me. Somewhere else. The sky as blue as a robin's egg, like blue through and through, nothing else in front or behind it. There are other things. I know there are. Hands in my pockets, I can feel the seams, the stitching, coming loose. I look back and there are other sites with little wisps of smoke coming off the morning fires. Coffee, bacon probably. Not us. Nothing warm for breakfast since the ranch. I remember Marianne, the cook, the oatmeal and scones she'd set out for the workers before she served the guests. Warm and warm and sweet with syrup and berries.

I think it's the Crazy Mountains for sure. I look down at my feet—high-top Vans. I might not make it over today, but I will. I am going to go. I just have to figure out where. Where I'm headed. Where I want to be.

IVY

I like to hold the rock when I'm on the phone. It has these strange relaxing properties. When my hand is too hot, it's cool. And when I'm cool, it warms me. I throw the rock in the air, catch it. Again.

"Alex texted," Claire says. "He wants to hang out."

I miss it now and it hits my desk with a delicate ping, falls to the sweet soft carpet. "Are you going to?"

"I don't know," she says. "I mean, why not, I guess."

"Do you even like him?"

There's silence.

"Do you?"

"I just love who he is, in the world. Like this big person."

"Do you want to make out with him or be him?" I ask.

"I don't know."

"I think you want to be him?" I say, and she focuses in.

This rock. I feel a desperation about finding her. It's different now. In my bones, I feel it. Under my skin. It makes me itchy and sore.

"I mean, he's kind of a dick," I say.

"But did you read those poems?"

I nod.

"Hey, so, me now. Are you up for that road trip?" I ask. "The find-my-birth-mom journey?"

"Absolutely," Claire says. I can tell she's thinking if she wants to be Alex.

"Okay, I'm calling Patrick now," I say. "More soon."

"More soon," Claire says. "More and more and more."

I think of leaving here, even for this trip. This, here, is not misery at all. I love my family, all our chickens, my grandmother who comes here and sighs into a chair and says to my mom, darling, when on earth are you coming home? Mom's been here for, what, twenty years? It's more home than the original home now. That's how I feel about it.

My mother always says, oh, Nelly, like her mother's name is a sigh.

But still, it's like, I want to know. Like I need to know what happened between then and now. Because . . . life.

I call up Patrick.

Swoop, hey, hi, what's up, done with practice, cool, yeah, I want to find my mother.

"You need to talk to your moms," Patrick says. "They love you, I."

The thought of leaving them makes me want to cry. Why would I leave them? And it's like a movie: Riding my new tricycle with streamers on the handles. My first puppy. My first cat. The first guinea pig. The visits to my grandmother in the city. Lying in bed with Mom when I'm sick. Her reading to me, all safe in her arms. My first day of kindergarten. The three of us looking out from the Eiffel Tower. Paris. Collecting shells in Maine. The day Pearl got mauled by a fox. Picking out Court and Spark, taking them home. Gay pride in New York City. The Pantheon in Rome when it started to snow. It's more like a photo album flipping through the years. My memory won't move like a video does. I have had this beautiful life, even I can see that. But there has been this thing and it has been missing. I am allowed to go looking for it. "I want to find her now."

"Let's go," says Patrick. "Let's do it."

"Claire wants to come, too."

Another pause. "Well then," Patrick says. "Road trip."

Patrick.

I put down my rock.

"Okay," I say. "It's just Ithaca. I mean, that's where she was."

"Let's start there," Patrick says. "A good place to start."

"Okay," I say again, and we are back to before. Good night, GG, Dt (done talking). Hang up. More texts come in but I am already texting Claire.

We are going, I type. *Let's go*, my thumbs say. *Let's find my first mom.*

BRIDGET

Nothing feels different inside, but I'm in the hospital now. It's over and I take her home. I don't look at the parents. I don't talk to my mother. I don't think about Baylor. I just take her. Maybe I convince myself it's so everyone can say good-bye. My family. My blood. Home.

I can't go into it. What it's like. You know her. You know her. You know her. And then it's like, isn't my body supposed to finish up here? After? After she's been cut from me.

Forget about during. I could remember forever about what it was like to deliver her. Maybe I am. Right now. Maybe these are my memories.

I can't get into any of it, not even to myself. But this: I take her home and I have nothing for her there because that wasn't the plan. No crib, no cute little onesies and booties for her teeny kissable toes. Just the little bag of baby crap they give you when you leave: a hand-knit cap, a pacifier, a can of formula, ten diapers. The blue-and-pink-striped blanket she's wrapped in. But I have me. I am her mother. My self finishing what my self started. I don't know what I'm thinking. I'm crazy with sadness. It's the most crazy sadness I've ever had in my life. I can't imagine it being like that again ever. Baylor dumping me? Please. That was a push in the lunchroom. This is a full-fledged thirty-car interstate pileup. This is an ax to the head, to the heart, a knife slashing at my throat. This is a thing you don't come back from the same. Maybe you don't come back at all.

If you come back. Do you? Do you? How do you know?

I take her home and I lock my door and my boobs are all filled up and I'm in there with her for a minute or seven months or sixteen years, I can't say. I don't take any calls. If it's the adoptive family, that's not the family anymore, I am. I am delirious with my choices. From them. There are so many and there are so few. All of them, those pink lines I dream about like they're swords from another time and someone is on a dragon charging at me with them. The lines turn into a baby. That's what happens in my dreams and that's what happens now.

I have a daughter I have a daughter I have a daughter.

I wake up from napping, lightly, I'm scared I will smother her, and I think first that I have a daughter and it's like finally waking up on Christmas, it really, really is. And then I remember all of it, and how if I keep her I will lose everyone.

I pray. I am a good person. Please, I am humble, please tell me what to do.

I need to know that what I'm doing is right. What is regret?

My mother bangs on the door but she doesn't say what a mother is supposed to say.

This is what a mother is supposed to say: I love you I love you I love you I will never ever let you go. You are not alone.

Why isn't my mother saying this? She is banging on the door.

She is saying, "So help me God, Bridget, if you don't give that child back, you will not be staying here."

"Give it back? Back? This is back. I am back."

"You will have to go," my mother says. "This was not the plan. Those poor people!" she is saying.

And who is she talking about? I know she means the parents. I know she means them—the lesbians she was once against—and not me and I can't care. No one can be hurting more than me.

"I need cream," I say, quiet. Ashamed. "For her."

"Honey," she says because she's not crazy. She knows. "Honey. Please. Your hormones are nuts right now. I'm telling you, come out. You cannot keep that child. It's all wrong now."

Which is when I think, who am I putting first? Here's this baby—what is her name? She's crying and crying. Secretly, I call her Sunny. I call her Lily. I call her Daisy. I call her Clementine. Aspen. Hazel. Anything that can grow. Everything between us is a secret. Her hot breath. Mine. Her fine sweet hair, the soft head, a spot I could jam my thumb straight through. I run my thumb along her forehead. Down her nose, just a little polka dot. Her belly, teeny hands, nails already growing and growing, fingers, long yummy toes. She eats and eats and if I can stay in here and never leave I will have everything I've ever wanted. Big love, heaven-sent love, all kinds of angels. If I don't move, I won't detonate my life. My life me me me. Will anyone love me again?

What about her?

What does it mean for her? What will she want who will she be what will she feel? What will she do without me? She cries a lot and I can't make her stop. She shits everywhere. I am running out of diapers and wipes and I don't have diaper cream, so I use the shea butter I was rubbing into my belly. Sometimes she won't eat, too, and also the crying changes. It's dark and deep and from her tummy I think and what if she's sick?

My body, too.

I want to put it all on the altar. I can do this.

I open the door and my mother is sitting out there, on the floor, back against the wall, hands propped on her knees, her head hung. There are diapers and wipes and a cream for her bum. My mother looks up to me.

"How long have you been sitting there?"

"Please," she says. "Bridget, please."

I hand her sunnydaisyjuneeverythingbeautifulinagarden. I sob. I feel like I will be sobbing like this for the rest of my days. I will be broken forever. "She's sick or something." I hiccup. "I don't know!"

My mother places my baby on her shoulder, tummy down, and lightly rubs her back. She's only wearing a diaper. I have nothing, no cute little onesies printed with flowers or monkeys or ladybugs to dress her in. No crib, no cradle. No Moses basket. But me. She has me. Her crying fades a little. Now it's a whimper.

"She's cold." My mother laughs. "And that's gas," she says. She holds her out in front of her for the first time. "It would be nice," she says to the girl. Mine. About to not be mine. "It would be nice because I love you I love you." Her face goes close to the baby's face. Her granddaughter's face.

I can't watch it. No one told me. Who would have told me?

My mother looks over my beauty to me. "Bridget, we have to do the right thing. For everyone. For this little girl." She gasped. "I didn't know this would be so hard."

"You didn't?" I say. "Didn't you have *me*?"

My mother walks down the hall now. And I know I have to surrender. I will answer the prayers of this family. I will. I will. They have been waiting. And who am I but one person? There are two parents. A big love. A house, a garden, trips to Europe, animals in cages, a piano. How, at my absolute best, can I be all that?

"Wait!" I scream. I follow her out. I take her sweet finger in mine. I kiss her nose.

There's my daughter's face looking over my mother's shoulder.

I want her with everything inside me. For one moment she stops crying and, suddenly, I am me, now, me again, only exactly who that was. But I'm so different now. I am all these things inside now. I could have been a mother. I could be a mother. Everything feels like a choice. I am going to be everything now. Watch me. Watch me eat and drink and dance and kick and scream and scream. Watch me watch me watch me you won't see anything real. I am a secret, your secret, watch me forget your name.

I realize, now, for the first time, it is over. It is done. The thing growing in me that was all mine, only mine, the thing I sometimes woke to think of like a present I could unwrap and who mostly I woke weeping when I remembered it, it's gone now.

She's gone. This is the story of a baby that never was, a story that has been erased from the story of our family. I know what I am doing. It's not a decision, really, it's just the way I do a lot of things now.

I will be something. I will be anyone.

I let her go.

PART 2

IVY

2017

"I don't think you should go," Mo says. She stands, and it feels like she's blocking my way.

We're on the deck; it's where everything happens around here, least when it's not wintertime. And here we are in spring. Spring break. Woo-hoo. Partay.

"Are you, like, blocking me, Mo?" I ask. "It's an hour away."

She withdraws. Sometimes she tries so hard to be bigger, she doesn't realize. Sometimes I know she has to. That's how she got listened to. But not today. No, sir, not right now.

"No, Ivy," she says, "I'm not blocking you; I'm just talking to you. And it's not the distance. There's a lot of psychic distance, too." She sits down and I watch her grab both of the arms of the wrought iron chair. She looks older to me suddenly. Weary. It makes me sad. Mo is fifty-seven.

"Psychic distance?"

I forgot to mention: Mo is a social worker.

"Because we had a plan," I continue. "You said I could go during break and here it is. Break. Spring." I point up to the blue sky. "Would you rather I head to Puerto Vallarta like the cheerleaders this year?" I fiddle with the locket, run it back and forth over its chain. It's cold around my neck. *Zzz* is the sound.

Mom watches me. I know she sees it. "Honey, no, stop, what Momo means is that we don't want you to go alone. It's a lot. The trip at your age is a lot, and with Patrick, and I'm just not that comfortable." She looks over at Mo.

"Well, maybe you should have thought of that when you were reading my mail."

"In 2012," Mo says, rising.

"And anyway, I'm going with Patrick and—"

Mo just ignores this and continues. "And Claire. That's for sure, you are not going alone with Patrick. But yes, maybe we should have thought about it while we were waiting at your ballet lessons and while we were throwing huge croquet parties on the lawn here? Or when your mom was sewing your Halloween costumes? Remember when you wanted to be a perfect Disney princess and even though I was against it because Disney is totally fascist your mom did it and then you decided, the day before, mind you, that you were too old for princesses and you wanted to be a carrot. Remember that? How Mom went out and bought all the crap you needed for your . . . carrotness . . . and she was up all night sewing for you. Maybe I should have thought of it then."

"You done?" I say.

"Yes," Mo says, gripping the arms of her chair. "I am."

Mom takes a deep breath. It's a sigh and a breath and it also seems kind of elderly.

"Last I checked that's what parents did. But I guess you're saying it's so unusual you know because I'm not really your kid."

There. I said it. I have never said it before but I am saying it now even though there is no part of me that is feeling it. I am saying it to cause as much damage as I can in proportion to what I want. I want to go.

Mom looks like she's been punched in the belly and Mo looks pissed as hell. She's getting all big and bulky again, and Mom lays a hand on her shoulder. "Okay," Mom says calmly. "That's enough. We will not dignify this with a response, Ivy. You can just sit with what you've said for as long as you like."

I sit. I look up at the sky. I look around me, and far beyond to the chicken coop. I think of the newest chicken, some kind of Polish breed I think; I named her Wilbur and I think she's beautiful. I am looking everywhere but I am not thinking about it.

Everyone is silent.

I feel awful. And I know I should say so, but I want to hurt them. I want them to be angry at me. I think that will make it easier for me to go looking for her. Without them.

Mo interrupts the silence, surprise, surprise. "We don't think you should go because you're sixteen years old and it could be excavating something very painful. That's what I meant, Ivy. Darling. I think you know how we feel about our family and about being your parents."

"But it's different," Mom says quietly. "It would be wrong to say that we don't think about the gift of you. You are ours one hundred percent, and if I could have had biological children with Mo I would have wanted to give birth to you. If you must know it is the one thing. I wish I could have had you, YOU, so we wouldn't be having this conversation. That is the only thing."

I look up at the sky. Blue blue blue.

"But we are," Mom continues, "and I didn't give birth to you and the young girl who had you—who was just your age—is out there. And you deserve to find her. And she deserves to see you, the amazing young woman that you have become."

I swallow. My throat is closing up. My moms. My family. I want no other way of being in the world. I want to be little again and in between them in bed on Sunday, Mo's popovers in the oven, reading *Charlotte's Web*, just the three of us, all of us the third girl, our toes all touching, before Charlotte dies, before I knew there was something else I had to do. Before before before. Remember that? Before everything. "I love you," I say, and I start sobbing. Sob-bing.

They both run over because, you know what? They will always think I hung the moon. That is the life I ended up with. It's complicated and it's so, so simple. But it's beautiful. They hug and hug me.

In these kinds of moments? It is only a story about being found.

They both stand up. Mom is shaking her head and wiping her hair out of her face—she has a witchy streak of white that is pretty dang cool—and she says, "Beauty."

"Just give me the address," I say.

They both nod their heads.

"Okay, then," Mo says. She hands over a slip of paper. "Here's where she used to live. This is where we met her."

It's an address in Ithaca, New York, not an hour from here.

"Is this where you met me?"

They both shake their heads but no one says anything. Mom's gaze kind of shifts off to the woods. Mo puts her hand on her leg.

Imagine, I'm thinking. Sixteen years and still that can make them go sad and silent and scared.

"That was a long time ago," Mom says. "And that's everything we have. I think when someone says don't look for me you might want to think about that."

"That was five years ago," I say softly.

Mo brushes her hands together. "There you have it."

Mom is still looking off the terrace, toward some horizon. I can tell they're sort of traumatized about this, but in a different way than I am. Because I am a little excited, too.

"I'm going," I say.

They both stay seated. No one gets up and tries to stop me or anything. It's not a movie here on our deck; it's just our lives.

"Okay," Mom says.

"Got it," says Mo.

Mom says, "I just want to be clear on something. We're not scared for us, Ivy. We're your parents. We know that with every-thing we are and we know you know that. We're not scared for us. Honey, we're scared for you."

"Duly noted," I say as I head back into the house to get my bag, the screen door—that sound of the past—slamming three times behind me.

JOANNE AND ANDREA

1996
Ithaca, New York

"Get up!" Andrea says, looking around. "We're in a restaurant!"

"I won't," Joanne says. "Not until you say you will. Need I remind you this floor is hard!"

Andrea looks down at her plate. Beside her a fire blazes as it had the first night they'd come here, just a year ago tonight. A ring lays sweetly on the white ceramic surface where there was once a chocolate molten lava cake. A simple gold band. She looks back up at Joanne, her wide green eyes staring up at her, filled with hope. "If only," Andrea whispers. "If only."

Joanne shakes her head. "Forget that." Her blond hair is cropped short and Andrea can see all the studs along her earlobe, catching the firelight.

Andrea places her hand at Joanne's cheek. "Get up. Please." She glances out the window. The snow outside, gathering in heaps.

Joanne leans on her leg and pushes herself up. She dusts herself off and sits back at the table, across from her love. The love of her whole life. She leans toward Andrea and her eyes glisten in the light. She leans her chin into her hands.

Andrea looks at Joanne's tapered fingers, her broad, cut nails.

Those hands. She picks up the ring.

"But if we could," Joanne says.

Andrea dunks her napkin in her water glass and cleans the band of all the chocolate sauce and cake. She goes to put it on her finger but Joanne reaches across the table and stops her.

Andrea looks up, startled. Perhaps she made her wait too long.

Joanne takes Andrea's left hand gently in hers and slides the gold band on her fourth finger. "My forever love," Joanne says. Her hands are dry and calloused from gardening.

Andrea looks hard at Joanne. They had come here, to this exact table, on their second date just one year ago. Snow outside and they'd drunk too much wine and had to walk home to Joanne's, twenty minutes down the road. That night there was a rising moon that had followed them all the way home. It had lit the way for them.

Andrea covers Joanne's hand with hers. "I do," she says.

Joanne is crying now. "One day," she says.

"One day soon," says Andrea, and they both turn to watch the fire crackling beside them.

IVY

2017

Waze says Ithaca is an hour from our town. I've got rock in pocket. *Intention I feel inventive*, I hear Chrissie Hynde boom. *Gonna make you, make you, make you notice* . . .

So. Here we are, Claire holding up her phone, which, in Boy Band voice is telling Patrick, *Left*, now *right*, now *stay straight*. Claire looks between the seats at me.

"She is straight!" she responds.

"Right on," I say. "But it is a continuum." I look over at Patrick's worried face and laugh.

"We're taking the back roads," she says. "Punch it!"

"There are no back roads," I say. "I mean it's all back roads. Here we are on Country Road 12. It's called *country road*. Have you ever even thought about that?" Our house hovers above it, above the lake. And behind us is all forest, right past our barn. Like I said, May to October, it's dreamy. Winter? The forest is like a fairy tale gone wicked in the winter, unless it's snowing. So are the city streets called City Street 12? I never saw it. We don't drive in the city. Gram shoots out her hand and, boom, *taxi*.

"Let's do Thirteen," says Patrick. "Straight shot."

Claire shrugs.

I fiddle with the radio. *I will become yours and you will become mine,* Sara Bareilles sings.

Patrick groans and moves to change it.

"Stop!" Claire and I both say it, together. We sway, me in the front, her in the back. We snap our fingers like it's old-school girl bands. Doop doop. Wop.

I choose you. I choose. You, yeah.

Patrick moves his hand from the dial and even though he's not looking at me, just by the lilt of his head I can tell he's rolling his eyes again. Want to say: careful or your eyes might stick that way, but it's not even funny as a joke I don't believe in. I don't know if he's smiling, but I do know that suddenly it hits me.

What if I find her?

I might find her.

I am not thinking: I might not find her because what would be the point of that?

Maybe this will be easy; maybe she'll just be there. Maybe that's where she's always been, as if she's been sitting in some chair waiting for me to arrive. I take the letter out of my bag, just to make sure I have not left it or dropped it or accidentally thrown it away, as if it will be proof of something. See? I will hold it out to her. I'm yours. It's like a valentine. Unfortunately I spend pretty much half my time checking to make sure I have stuff—phone in particular, obviously—and thinking I lost stuff. Here I go: oh my God, where is it, you guys?, I can't find it, the letter!, fuck, we have to go back, you guys!, oh, right, here it is, the letter is here. I pat my bag. *Hanging with my gnomies,* it says, one of Mo's gardening totes.

Here it is, thank you, Goddess.

From the back, Boy Band tells Patrick to get off the highway.

"Here!" Claire screams, head between the front seats, when he doesn't go to exit.

"Why didn't you tell me?" Patrick swerves off. "I, like, zone out with that app. It's ridiculous."

"Dude! I'm telling you now."

Patrick slides me a look. What does his look say? It's a lot of things: like Hello, love, and also, Seriously?, and I wish we were alone. It's also angry, and mostly it's a look that says, I know you, person freaking out over a letter somewhere in the bottom of your bag, from a ghost.

I catch his eye, and then I look away.

"You alive?" Claire asks me.

I break into a smile. "I'm alive," I say.

I lean back.

"Here I am."

Claire starts yelling directions and then we're headed in and out of little neighborhoods. There are—pretty shockingly—three Eagle Lanes, so, though it turns out we want 3476 Eagle Pass, we turn into a lot of them. Even with GPS it's amazing how many driveways you can turn around in. Like, what did people do before? Were they just always . . . lost?

It's so hard to tell about things in towns like this, all our upstate towns. The address is north of Ithaca proper, and we continue on the highway. In a way, everything looks awful. Buildings are crumbling along the highways and huge factories are empty, their windows shot through. What if she has been here? Like the whole time? So close to me.

As we pull off, there are rusted things piled up in people's yards and roof beams are rotting. And also there is green grass and the trees are coming in with leaves. There is all kinds of space just out of town, too. You can't tell where bad stuff happens or where the rich people live. It's just all . . . here. And finally, at the end of a long dirt road, Eagle Pass, we're at a house. It says 347. There is a dark outline where the 6 must have once been. It's just a shadow now.

I can tell rich people do not live here. It's not that kind of long road. Let me rephrase: there are blue tarps instead of windows and the steps up to the front door are rotting through. There are some old busted-up cars outside. It's what Mom would call a ranch-style house, as in a rectangle, boring. There are some lawn chairs outside, too, that look like they never got taken in for the winter. But it's this kind of glorious sunny day and there is a load of green here and it's spring and I swear birds are singing when we step out of the car and shield our eyes from the sun.

I'm thinking: my moms were here once. Was this old Chevy out there then? I'm thinking, were there regular windows? What had my moms thought walking in? Or maybe, I think, this was beautiful wood back then.

Obviously the people here are in trouble, I don't mean to be unkind, but it is freaking me out because what if she's here?

I can see curtains on one of the windows that still has a glass pane, one that faces out onto the front yard. The curtains are faded yellow, but it could be pretty faded, like washed in lavender a lot and hung in the sun, printed with some kind of flower, I can't say, or scary horrible faded, like been there too long, never washed, unloved. This is what I'm saying. What are we stepping into? Lavender faded flowers or a documentary from social studies?

Claire takes my hand. So does Patrick. We walk to the front door. We take this big collective breath, like we are one person.

I try to twist my face into a smile and I can feel it forming, as if I am making it out of modeling clay.

We let go of each other's hands. We shift our feet.

Here we go.

I knock.

We all wait.

Nothing.

I knock again. And again.

Nothing.

And then: we hear it. Shuffling and hacking coughing and then the door cracks open. "Can I help you with something?" A very fragile very old woman with age spots across her face and scalp, which I can see through a layer of very thin hair, cracks open the door. Her pink scalp shines through the layer of yellowish-white hair.

My first thought is that she is a ghost. It's like I can see through her.

I peer in and I can tell in one look that she is human and those curtains are not flowered. The smell of cigarette smoke and maybe a few cans of soup that have been opened for, say, three years, and old wet dog breath smacks me in the face.

I can hear our sociology teacher, Mr. Engles, saying: "The number of rural Americans living in poverty is at thirteen percent."

"What?" she says when we are all sort of stunned silent.

"Children," Mr. Engles says, "make up a disproportionate share of our country's poor."

Patrick says, "We're looking for someone who used to live here. Maybe still?"

I nod, dumbly, like an idiot, frankly. What if this person is my grandmother, say. Or great-grandmother. This is what I am thinking and I can't stop myself from thinking that one day I might look like this. These could be my *genes*. Then again, we all might look like this one day. Right? I look at Claire. Even Claire. But not Mom. She has this, like, I don't know, handsome quality about her. I can't imagine her ever looking like this lady. Which makes me sad that I'm not biologically related to Mom. My beautiful, sweet mom. I miss her.

Claire steps up. "Yes, from about sixteen years ago. How long have you been here?"

"Me? Not more than ten, honey. Not more than ten. My nephew rents this place. But he never lived here. I had to leave. . . ."

"I see," Claire says. "Do you remember who was here before?"

"Who are you? It's a lot of questions from a stranger, honey."

I could tell she was trying to be nice. But what did we look like to her in our new jeans and long pretty hair and our teenageness? With our shiny Subaru Outback at the end of her drive?

"Friends of the previous owners?" Patrick says, and I get why he makes it a question.

"Owners?" she says.

"Residents?" says Patrick.

"No," she says. Her hands, her knuckles, huge with knots, are holding the door tight. She doesn't want us in. And you know what? That's just fine with me. "Never met the previous tenants. I remember they left a lot of crap here, though," she says, her body rattling with a cough.

"What kinds of things?" I ask.

"Lord if I remember. A lot of clothes. The daughter, she was in some kind of trouble. Drugs maybe. Or some kind of law thing. I don't now recall."

"Drugs?" Patrick says.

"Law thing?" Claire asks.

Relief courses through me and I am ashamed. I would rather my birth mother be run out for drugs or some kind of law thing than share DNA with this person. Whose only crime, far as I can tell, is being old and not in control of her finances. I do know what that says about me and can't help it.

"I have no idea but they seemed to be leaving town for good. That was a lifetime ago now. I was still working and—"

"Thank you," Claire says. "Any forwarding address? Did they leave anything like that?"

"Forwarding address?" There was a little cackle. "Honey, hell if I know. I had my own troubles then. Still do. You're standing on some of them," she says, and we look down, shift our feet on the rotting wood of the steps. "Dump," she says.

We nod, sort of stunned, because to be honest I've never seen people living like this. I've seen it on television, but that is mostly footage of people after disasters or people in other countries being forced to leave. So close to home, this is. So close. And again, I feel that wave of shame.

But I still can't wait to get out of here and so we thank her and we stumble down her slippery rotten steps and we get in the car again. We are silent as we pull out. *Turn left!* says Boy Band, and I just want them to be turned off because it all seems messed up now. It's not fun anymore. *Another left!* they trill because I can't figure out how to do it. Turn them the hell off. *Stay straight*, they say and the joke is just so over and I scream at Claire to please for the love of God make them shut up.

Riiight, says Boy Band, and Claire shuts them off and no one says anything as Patrick shifts into second, then third, and, without asking, takes us onto the highway, fast.

It's cold for spring, even for up here. I can feel the temperature dropping and I feel sort of scared. I'm scared that I didn't bring warm-enough clothes, just a light fleece and a jean jacket, but also scared of everything. Like, the world seems like a very scary place to me. One second I'm all, let me out at you, world, stop holding my hand, and then the next it's like, let me go home and crawl into my bed beneath my warm down comforter and my soft gold silk blanket.

"That was weird," is what I say as we drive. Trees flank the highway. Like they do everywhere.

I see Patrick nod and his eyes search again for mine.

"That's one way of putting it," Claire says.

I feel other things, though. Aside from the gratitude that that lady is not related to me. Aside from being ashamed that I did not know how much less people had, so close to me. But other things, deep inside, like: I might not want to know. Her. Maybe she said don't find me for a good reason. Maybe all these things are for a reason. I feel the rock in my pocket, just jabbing me in my hip. Everything hurts a little bit.

When you're not adopted, there are things you don't know. You accept it, the way we all accept that no one knows when it will be over, say. When your grandmother will die, or your dog. When you will even. It's going to happen to us all sometime. If I were related to that lady in that horrible house with the horrible smell, would that make anything different to me?

Well, it would. Because I would know that person has passed something down to me. Through blood. I don't know, though, what that would be. I am still me. The same person I was before I met her. I am so much more me than my blood and all those genetics.

"I hope that lady is going to be okay," Patrick says.

We are all silent. We all feel the asphalt of the road beneath us. We all see the trees whipping by.

Who knows how much time has passed when Claire says, "I could really use something with whipped cream and caffeine," she says. "Let's see, a good café. Closest café, Siri," she says, and we are turned around and headed off the highway. This little building hangs over a creek. It's almost like it used to be a house.

No one's in the lot. I peer inside and I see that no one's in there, either. It's all closed up, all the chairs turned over on tables, the paintings—of different birds in nests—knocked crooked.

I look over at Claire. "Can you get your girly coffee in town?" I ask.

Patrick laughs.

"You know you want the same thing," I say to him.

We trudge back to the car and Patrick puts "Town" into Waze and Boy Band starts up again. *Leeeft,* they say.

I hate them.

There's a common lined with stores and cafés and Patrick looks for parking. I've been here a couple of times before, with my moms. There is a famous Buddhist sanctuary here, and sometimes Mom used to go for the afternoon. Mo and I would wander around and eat mushy vegetarian food or go hiking at the Falls nearby. Butterpeak. It all looks so familiar to me, but also, so foreign. Like a town I've seen in books or something. A place I was in in another life.

Patrick parks and we head toward the Commons by foot. There's a café on the corner and the three of us go in and order hot chocolates with lots of whipped cream and then we go sit down on stools looking out at the street and dip our faces into the steam and watch the people in the town move around. College students. White girls with dreads. (Seriously bad idea.) Old men professors in corduroy jackets. Hikers. A lot of hippies. A man in a pickup pulls into a spot on the street in front of us, hauling all kinds of wood and also copper wire, and he looks so familiar but I cannot place him. A white guy with dreadlocks (worse than the girls) walks into the café and orders something complicated.

Patrick says, "What if that had been your grandmother?"

I look at him. Like, stare at him. There's stink eye in my stare. There's a lot of other things, too, but I can't really name them.

"I just feel sad," I blurt out. I start to cry.

Claire takes my hand under the counter. Patrick takes my other hand. I have no free hand to drink my chocolate, so I just lean in and lick at the whipped cream.

"We haven't even started yet," Claire says.

Patrick nods. "We'll find her. It's, like, our mission now."

The man in the pickup has a paunch and a toothpick in his mouth, a wool hat because spring is like a lie here. He secures a lot of stuff on the back of his truck. There's a woman in the car with him—black black hair. She turns to throw her bag in the back and I can see her pretty face. He opens the door and Alicia Keys streams out: *Some people want diamond rings.*

They're right. We haven't even begun.

I want to go home but I don't say so. "Why do I even want to find her? I just want to have a look at her and then go home."

Claire's head is bobbing. "Get that," she says. "Just a peek, right? And then have everything be the same."

It hurts me to think of things changing. Of me changing them. But it's so hard to not know.

"Want to walk around?" Patrick asks. "I saw a used bookstore up there."

Claire and I nod.

"Then we'll go back?"

I nod again. Back is fine with me. Back and back and back.

As we're walking into the old bookstore—dust, paper, weird wood smell. Kind of like Patrick's house, actually. I don't know why but I always go first to the children's section in bookstores. I just love the picture books—all the colors and the wide-open happiness of the covers. My moms read to me all the time. Books remind me of being young and safe, before I knew anything. Also, they're like my memories. Here we go: Pickles the fire cat. Harry the dog. Frog and Toad, Curious George. All the animals of being a little girl.

The girl in the bookstore with her nose ring and her shaved head, she doesn't talk to us. I secretly love her. Patrick goes with me and Claire, always looking for a new cover of the magazine, goes predictably to art, but I can't blame her: we don't have a store like this in our town, all wood and high rafters and everything you want just on the shelf, even things you never knew.

I can see her looking at these massive photo books. Then she takes out a smaller paperback and thumbs through it.

We slide out a book with a llama in red pajamas on the cover and I think of that old lady in her boarded-up falling-down house. I wonder was she cold all winter? Did anyone look after her? I wonder what it looked like when my first mom lived there. The stupid llama makes me laugh.

Claire holds up her book. "*New York Foundlings, 1950–1970!*" Claire screams. "This is so great!" She calls me over. "Foundling. I just love this term. Don't you? Can we change *Crossroads* to *Foundlings?*"

"Foundlings?"

"You know, orphans," she says.

I can't tell if she is being insensitive on purpose or just totally clueless. The word bothers me. Like really bothers me. "No," I say. "We can't."

"Okay, how about *The Foundlings*? Everything sounds better with a the in front of it, doesn't it?"

"No," I say.

"Okay, but just look at these kids," she says to no one. "Any one of these would be an awesome cover."

I want to strangle her.

I don't care about the cover of *Crossroads* right now. Or any of the poems either. I'm standing there watching the shaved-head woman, her fingers covered in rings, *rings on her fingers*. . . . Mom used to bounce me up and down and sing that.

It's like I've conjured her because just as I am about to say something to Claire about the upsetting book she seems to have no idea is sad and upsetting, my phone rings and it's her, Mom.

"Hey."

"Hi, honey, how are you?"

"Good," I say.

"Anything else you want to offer? I'm not asking about the weather after all."

"Well, she wasn't there, if that's what you mean."

I can hear her breathing but she doesn't say anything.

"At the house."

"I see," my mother says.

"You knew that, didn't you?" I asked her. I feel so angry. But

I don't know if it's at her or not.

"No, Ivy. I didn't know that. I suspected it, but I didn't know it."

I feel like I will cry. I want to weep right now. I step out of the bookstore and the little bell rings behind me. *Bells on her toes* . . .

"There was this terrible old lady there!" I say. "And it was an awful old house. It was disgusting." I virtually wail this. I feel bad because it's not how I would normally talk about that house or that woman but it just comes out that way.

"I'm sorry, Ivy." Mom is getting upset, I can tell. For me. I know she is upset for me. "Come home. We will figure out another plan."

I'm sniffling. "Yeah? How?" That last bit comes out like a howl. I can hear myself but I can't stop myself. I wipe the snot off on the corner of my sweater, look in and watch Patrick and Claire through the window in their separate sections. Patrick's head is bowed toward the picture books, still, and Claire moves to the register to pay for her foundling book. The girl/woman goes to ring her up without even looking at her.

"Come back. We will all figure this out together," Mom says.

"Okay," I say. "We're coming," I say as I open up the door to go back inside.

IVY

2017

Patrick drops Claire off first, even though it's totally out of the way, and then he pulls into my driveway, which is long, packed dirt, framed by trees. Now the branches look like those old lady's brittle fingers, but in early summer they are magic. I used to ride my bike beneath the cave of leaves and think I was in some kind of fairy tale.

I am in a fairy tale. Anybody's happy ending.

It's nighttime now. I can hear the swallows swooping in and soon the wings of the bats from the woods will start flapping, all of those night things that take place that we can't see or know about. It's the in-between time now, though, and I can feel all the things changing from light to dark. I can't explain it. It's a happy time and a sad time that time of the day. The gloaming. The gloaming, a word I love. It's a word I will use forever and ever until I die because I think it's a romantic word and I love it.

Patrick turns off the car and the lights and he looks over at me, in the front seat, hands in my lap.

Patrick. Last year when we started, it was in English. Patrick sat behind me. As Mr. Lewis read, his long, hairy fingers keeping the book open, the covers furled back, and Patrick would draw on my scalp. Gave me goose bumps. "I'm writing our names," he would say and I'd feel the sharp "I" that starts my name.

He's all in, but right now it's not boo or bae or hey-ho kk how goes it, Nuffer, another name I've got from how I love Marshmallow Fluff and Nutella, but it's this fierce searching look. He leans in. There is barely any light and there is the sound of the ticking of the engine, still hot. His hand is at my chin and he guides my face to his. He kisses me.

It's different than our usual kissing, which I only understand is happening when he presses harder with his lips. He brings his arms around me and he makes a little tiny noise, like part sigh, part whimper. Not too much that it's disgusting, just a little sound to tell me, I think, that he loves me. This.

I kiss him back and as I do I realize I am kissing Patrick like I mean it. It's almost like it's the first time I have ever meant it. I am kissing him about this day, which means I am kissing him as a different person because I am changed. And he was there. And we did this hard, sad thing together. I lean back a little bit and he is sort of leaning into me now, not hard or anything, but I feel his body, his slender kind of lanky Patrickness on me. The seat belt thingie is at my head and the chain of my locket is kind of strangling me, but I don't make a joke about that or anything else because that will end this and also, I hold him, too, just as tightly, just as hard, because I am here, too, now. We are the same now. And then.

And then! The house light switches on and I can see Mo opening the door, looking out into darkening yard.

"I?" she calls. "Ivy?"

I can see Court beside her, also looking out to the yard.

Patrick gets up, creaking like an old person, and I sit up and clear my throat and straighten out my sweater, picking off invisible things as if we've been rolling in fallen leaves.

"Hi," he says, pulling on my sleeve.

I don't even care it's the snot sleeve from earlier. I nod, not looking at him.

"Hi, my intense girlfriend."

I look at him. I like his nose. I like his sweet face. "Thanks for today," I say. I tilt my head to my left shoulder, make a smile frown. I open the car door. "Bye, Patrick," I say, and then I head toward my house. Toward home.

IVY

2017

It's Mom who takes me to the closet. It's where she used to hide all the Christmas and Hanukkah gifts. (Mom is Christmas, Mo is Hanukkah. So it's latkes and noodle kugels and menorah lights and then it's trees and wreaths and mistletoe and hand-knit stockings.) The closet is where she put all the stuff from her grandparents that she didn't want to lose but had no place for. Like silver shoehorns and letter openers and bracelets dangling with golden charms. Also, the summer clothes in winter. The winter clothes in summer. So it smells like things that don't belong in the real world anymore. And it sounds like tissue paper and plastic crinkling whenever you step inside.

The day after I get home from Ithaca, after I lie in bed with Mom like I haven't done for years, and Mo makes popovers downstairs, huffing and puffing like she's preparing the most complicated of meals for the most ungrateful of eaters, Mom says, "I'm going to show you everything."

Downstairs there is the clatter of Mo getting down the glass ramekins that, far as I can tell, are used only for this purpose. Popovers. I wonder which hens have provided the eggs this time—random thought but I think about it often—and Mom opens one of the old wooden bureau drawers.

I don't know what I expect to see there. Like a drawer heavy with stuff. Dolls, maybe, I have no idea why, like maybe she played with dolls?, and framed photos, maybe, a sheaf of letters tied with ribbons, boxes of acorns and pinecones and pressed flowers and leaves, roses maybe, still smelling like roses, too, all stuff from where my first mom grew up.

Mom rustles some tissue paper and what there is is none of those things. What there is is a scrapbook. It's small. Like one of those ones that seem to be like the babies of big albums and just features the stars of those massive adult books. Mom hands it to me.

I take it in two hands like it's a crown or a bowl of hot soup.

I look at Mom now because she is saying that's it but I don't think that's it.

Mom nods toward it.

"That's it?" I ask finally. I look down at the leather-bound book.

Mom closes her eyes and sighs. She swallows, miserably. "Yes, it is. There are two more letters in there."

I'm astonished. My parents have been all about honesty and truth, like, my whole life. They would say absurdly annoying things like "you die if you lie" and "the truth will always set you free." And then there is the issue of the previous letter, as if this was not problem enough. I start to tell her a louder version of this when she pre-empts me.

"Before you get self-righteous and angry, which I understand you must be, let me tell you something. One of the letters is

to us. It is not to you. It is not meant for you. It is to Joanne
and me, and I just wasn't sure it really was for you to see. I will
explain when I tell you after we received that one—about two
years ago—another one came following it."

"Following it?" It's like she's giving some kind of formal lec-
ture.

"Yes, Ivy, okay, like recently, okay? Several months ago. And
it said 'Please don't open until Ivy is eighteen.' And so we didn't.
We tried to respect that. So there is a letter, to us, which is
opened, and there is a letter, to you, for when you turn eighteen,
which you are not, not yet anyway, and it is sealed."

I feel like I'm going to pass out. How can I argue with such
waterproof logic? I try to imagine it. "So you just didn't give
them to me," I say lamely, still voicing my protest. I remember
marching for something or other on the commons in Ithaca,
high on Mo's shoulders when I was a little girl.

I wish I could explain how miserable my mother looks as she
tries to backpedal here. "I have tried to never say the things to
you that my mother has said to me. Remember my father died
when I was so young. He was this wonderful open person, at
least that's how I remember it, but my mother? She was hard. I
have tried to never say the things that drove me crazy or didn't
seem real, or didn't feel like they were coming from the right
place. I have worked very hard to be the kind of mother to you
that I would have wanted. And maybe that's selfish. Maybe that's
not the kind of mother you wanted, you want, I know you are
not me, Ivy, but in any case, that's been my intent. Always. To
be better. To be good. To be good for you and protect you when

you need protecting and to let you go when you need to be freed. It's hard to know sometimes which is which. Like, when to lock the doors tight and when to throw them open."

I am looking at my mother. My beautiful mother. Who has lines around her eyes now, delicate and fine as a spider's silk threads. Along her mouth, too. Sometimes her lipstick bleeds into the lines and it makes me a little sad, mostly because I don't think she realizes it.

"But I need to tell you there are some things you just can't understand until you're older. How complicated this is." Mom swallows. No lipstick today. "Can we get out of this closet, please?" she asks.

"Ha," I laugh. "You there in the closet, gay lady."

"Hardly," she says grimly. "That is one thing I am sure of."

In any case I nod and duck my head and move out of the tiny threshold. We go back into my moms' room and I sit on the edge of their bed. I hold the album. I'm shaking so much it's practically vibrating on my lap. Mom sits down next to me but she doesn't try to touch me or anything, thank God.

She can't look at me. "I just want to explain something. How do I know what will hurt you and what will help you?" She looks at me now, and tears are streaming down her face. "I want you to find her, to meet her. And I want you to have everything you want. I'm not worried or jealous. I want her to meet you. And see what an amazing daughter she has! But I don't know what the best thing is for you all the time. The letter for us? I don't know, it was hard to read for us, and while I didn't throw it away, I thought I'd give it to you eventually, but I just didn't feel I needed to do it now. Mo, too. I don't just mean I, I'm just speaking for me now, but we're in agreement. Not always, but on this, we are in agreement."

I want to read the letter but I can tell I need to listen to my mother.

"And the second letter, it said 'Don't open' and we didn't. And we didn't because this is a girl who gave us the most important thing in the history of the world as far as your mom and I are concerned and that gift cost her. I know it has cost her a lot. She thought placing her child for adoption was the best thing for you and the best thing for her, but I'm not sure it was the best thing for her and I'm not sure, frankly, if I want to know everything because I'm scared."

Mom is crying hard now. The only time I ever saw her cry this hard was when an old friend of hers from growing up had died. Gram had known her mother and called to tell her the news. My mother had cried like this, like the way she is crying now.

"And you," she says. "I am sure it has cost you, too. There are all kinds of loss. I know this, every day. And I want to protect you," she says.

I am thinking about what I've lost. A whole family. My whole family. It is overwhelming to think about and I imagine it: her meeting my birth dad. My only dad. Where was it?

Mom is still talking. "But I want to protect her, too, and I guess I want to protect me and Mo, too. I just don't want anyone else to be hurting! Ivy"—she looks at me with this fierce kind of intensity I thought was saved for, like, female soldiers, old-school warriors maybe—"before you was nothing. After you was

everything. So what if it was the opposite for her? How could
it not have been the opposite for her? I don't want you or me to
have to know all that."

She takes a big intake of breath and lets it out and it's some jagged stuff, that breathing. Mo calls up from downstairs. "Hello?"
she says. "Syrup or honey or butter?"

Mom ignores her and Mo doesn't pursue it. I think of a girl
my age pregnant with me. But I can't because it's so out of my
realm. Even if I start having sex with Patrick in earnest, which I
might, I mean, it will happen, won't it? It's just ludicrous because
I can't imagine that leading to, well, me. I guess she hadn't realized that either.

I open the mini scrapbook. There are things like hospital
bracelets and, yes, pressed flowers. Medical papers with my
weight and my height. And lists of all the times I took a poop
and how much I ate. There is the photo I have, of all of us in the
hospital. All girls. Girl army.

But who is the third girl? I guess it was the first mom.

The letters are in the back. I flip the pages over in one go and
pull them out.

"You let me go to Ithaca and you knew she wasn't even there?"

Mom shakes her head. "No. When you read it you'll see. I
had no idea what she was doing. She easily could have gone back
home."

One envelope is carefully opened, as one can only do with a
proper letter knife that of course Mom has, and I can see a slip of
writing paper peeking up from inside. The other is a plain white
envelope. It's addressed to my mothers and there is no return

address. On the back, across the seal, it says *For Ivy, when she turns 18*. I can see it will be hard to open. It's like looking in someone's diary, isn't it? I think. It's this mad violation that I am even holding it.

But I am. Holding it. I put it aside and slip the letter out of the envelope that has been opened. Shaking, I unfold it.

January 19, 2014
Dear Andrea and Joanne,
I know that I broke my promise to you. I'm not sure if you care or not. Maybe you're relieved that I left, I can't say because even though I gave you my child I don't really know you very well. That came out wrong. I know you are great parents. I just don't know if me leaving your lives is something that feels good or bad for you. How could that be? That I don't know more. But I do know I broke my promise to be there and to see my daughter grow up. I know she is your daughter. I am not confused or coming for her or anything like that but she is also still a little bit mine, too.

I will start with thank you. For raising my beautiful child. For being the parents I couldn't be. For showing up and, even when I couldn't make up my mind, for sticking with me. It's a thank-you for all you did for me before the birth—for the talks we had and for the cash and the nice clothes, and even for the offer of school, which I never did take you up on, did I? I made some dumb decisions, let me tell you.

I feel like you guys were a little bit like my mothers, too, so thank you for that. Also I want to tell you that I was always so glad you were two women. I didn't know how to say it. Because I was still very churchgoing at that time, I mean, it is how I grew up, it's why we're all here, isn't it? And so people were surprised I placed Ivy with you. First they were "surprised" I got pregnant, but then they were "surprised" that it was you two I decided on. But I just knew it when I saw your faces in that profile. And I have always been so glad, so deep-down happy, that it is women who are raising her. For too many reasons to go into here, now. Just a feeling I have.

I gave up my daughter because it was best for her but it was best for me, too. I thought I would have my whole life back and it would be like this had never really happened. Like I could erase it and start over, be better even, but I was not better. I did things I regret to make myself feel better and so I was not better or second chanced or anything like that. I ran away from what happened and so I had to run away from you both. I thought you would be so disappointed and I couldn't bear it. And I could not face my child.

I left everyone and I think you all would have cared the most. No one knew where I was. But now I am working to be someone for myself and for her and, yes, even for you both, and even for other kids, kids like I was and kids not like me at all. I've got my life back now, so I can tell you I was in a dark place but there is light now. That's the song, right? There is a crack in everything / that's how the light gets in. *I wasn't really one to listen to that kind of music, but I worked on a ranch with someone who loved that singer and she played him day in and day out as we brushed those horses, and fed them, washed them down. The horses loved him, too.*

Here now is the light. I don't know if you are still at this
address, but if you are, I hope this reaches you. I hope you too are
in the light. All the love and light.
    Your friend,
    Bridget

I look up and Mom is literally staring at my face, as if I am the
letter and she is trying to read me. I don't know what I am about
to do. It turns out that is me turning to my mother and crying.
Sobbing, really; I throw myself against her. I don't even know
why I'm crying. I feel bad for this person but I also know she's
not my mother. She is my mother but she isn't. She was first.
And there were all her people, too. Who are they?

I will say this: there is always a part of me that feels unwanted.
It's just the way it is, no one can argue it away or scrub it off me. I
don't know if this letter does anything to undo that, but it makes
me think other things about it. Like how it might not have had
much to do with me. Which is another conversation.

"Remember that she did the most wonderful thing," Mom
says. "A very selfless thing and I'm sorry you have to know that
she paid the price."

I do sort of wish I hadn't read it. I don't know why yet. I need
to, as Mo says, process it. I am scared shitless of the other letter,
though, I can tell you that. Maybe I will wait, like it says, until I
am a legal adult. Will I be different then?

"So I have been doing some research," Mom says. "When we
got the letter we tried to find her and we couldn't. I do remember

her saying she wanted to go back to school. And she always told us she wanted to go to New York City, which was the big city for her, for all of us, but I mean, that would be the city she would choose, I think. I can't say. But we can try to find her that way, on our own. And if not, we can hire someone to find her."

Mo stands at the door, huffing. "My popovers are falling," she says. "Did no one hear my cries? The are *deflating*."

I look up at her. She has flour on her nose and on her shoulder. Egg or melted butter plastered to her face. I can't help myself; I start to laugh. Mom laughs, too, and just as the two of us start laughing, Mo's face sort of turns because I can tell she's figured out what we're doing.

She pushes up her glasses with her ring finger. Now they have flour on them, too. "Thanks for letting me know you were having a moment," Mo says. "I mean, thanks for including me."

Mom is still laughing but she stops. Like sobs, laughter fades. "It was impulsive, I'm sorry."

I can tell there is, like, a pointed look being thrown in Mo's direction. Because it is nearly literally received by Mo, who nods.

"But we talked about it, right?" Mom says brightly to Mo while looking at me.

"Absolutely. Same page here! Let's go eat," she says. She goes to put her hand on the small of Mom's back, but then she stops. I think she realizes there will be flour. Or maybe she's upset at her.

Either way, we go downstairs and it all smells like cinnamon and sugar and butter and like my home and Mo turns on her folk music. I still feel the hiccupping sadness of that letter, of not being able to have read it earlier, of reading it now, of not being wanted, ever, and being so wanted, always, and Nanci Griffith, Mo's fave, sings: *For who knows where the time goes? Oh, who knows where the time goes?* And I can tell both my parents are feeling her, jagged and deep. Everyone is messed up today, all our hearts, what can I say. We listen, don't talk much. What do you say when it's just everything? I love them. But there are all kinds of questions. I down three popovers and then go upstairs to finally start to try to answer them.

I hadn't even known the questions.

Lansing, New York. Spring, summer.

You. You were sixteen. You were crying all the time. Right? Did I ever hear you laughing? You were wearing baggy clothes, you must have. Did people look at you and smile or did they look away? Did you talk to me? Sing to me? What did you sing? Or did you pretend I didn't exist? What kind of music did I hear you listening to while you ignored me? Who were the voices around me? Your friends? Your parents? We were growing together then. We had to be.

There was a time when I was growing, before I was me. I have forgotten these were questions. The beforeness. It has always been: what do you look like, sound like, what do you do, who are you? I forgot the questions about what we were in that time when we were together. When we were one.

Then: autumn and there I arrive with the changing leaves, a burst of all kinds of violent colors, changing. I am a problem that needs solving. I have been solved. There was a solution. Was there a solution?

They took me away. You gave me away.

Everyone loses their memories then.

A boy and a girl, my *parents*, fell in love. How does that work? He came with flowers? She wrote him letters? How do you fall in love? Or fall into love. How do you fall out of it? Because before I was with her they were together. Who were they?

Before before. These are questions, too.

I take out the letter for when I'm eighteen. It's got something else inside, like an old-fashioned prize from an old-fashioned cereal box. But I can't open it. Not yet. Instead, I go online. Again. I have done this before. Many times. *We Connect People*, the site says as it always has. You need to be over eighteen is another thing it always says.

For the purpose of this search, which best describes you? Scroll down.

This time I choose it: *I am the adoptive mother.* I click.

Enter a personal message. We would advise you not to share contact information such as your email or phone number until you verify a match! it says.

I am wondering if you are on here, Bridget. We have been look-ing for you. Ivy would like to meet you one day. I am wondering where you are now. We are sending love.

That is what my mother sounds like, I can hear her voice like I can hear my own even if the sound of it is different. And then I press return and wonder where my mother's voice goes.

Because I have not indicated any contact information, I have to check the site directly to see if there is a response. I'm not sure how it works. If she's on there, is she checking it, too? Or has she given her information up? Have they let her know that I—or my mom, this "Andrea"—has contacted her?

I wait until after dinner to check the site. And when I do, there is a response waiting for me. I see the red dot, the unreadness of this message, and I don't know what to do. I have lied. What will this person be saying to me? I go get the rock, my talisman now, and I gather up what is left of my shredded heart and I take deep breaths and then I do it: I click on the link to the message.

We have received your message. Thank you for using Adoption Registry, the official adoption finding site. We hope you have some communication soon!

Just another case of getting myself all worked up for nothing. So much so when I check the next morning and the red dot appears again, I think nothing of clicking on it, that it will be an update of the non-search that is happening in some database somewhere in the belly of my planet. And so I don't think and I don't work myself up or psyche myself up or chant anything or grab her rock and I don't really prepare for anything and of course that is the time that when I click on there is the message.

From her.

Here it is.

She is out there. She is looking. She is so close and still so far away.

Patrick honks three times from inside his mother's teal-green Subaru Outback and I am out the door.

Mom and Mo wave to me from the front steps. I know if this were any other road trip, one made up of fun and fun only, say, there would be no way in hell I'd be allowed to go. But rules are strange things when it comes to this stuff, right? Like, how can they tell me no? Now. After stealing my mail, which is, by the way, a federal offense? They can't tell me no.

In part, because I lied. I hated to do it. I have never lied. Fibbed, maybe. Said I brushed my teeth when I hadn't. That I hadn't eaten all the Tate's in the cookie bin. But this?

I showed them the email response from her, well, part of the response: *It's so nice to hear from you. I'm in school at NYU. Finally, school. And I'm in the classroom three days a week now. Teaching! I'm going to be a teacher. Hopefully. It would be great to see you!*

Mo's hand shook as she read the printout and Mom wiped away tears. But what they said, eventually, after a good deal of my pleading, was: you have two days there. "Two. Back on

Saturday." Mo had held up her hands, all but her index finger wrapped with silver rings.

"And you go to Gram's first and you leave the car there," Mom had said.

"Patrick can drive!" I had said.

"Not in Manhattan, he cannot," Mom had said. "No way, no how."

Mom couldn't help but smile, though. New York City. I wonder how much she misses it, really, because she says she misses *not one thing*. I don't really get the whole city thing. I don't get its big strange hazards or its massive appeal. It's just another place, another way.

"Okay," I had said. "God."

"And you go back there by nine pm. To Gram's. All right? Ivy, I am serious. This is not a joke. It's not safe. I will give you money for taxis and that is what you are to do. Are you sure you don't want me to come? I will be totally quiet! I will not speak for two days."

"Nine!" I had said. "What the hell, Mom?"

"What the hell to you, Ivy," she'd said. "Aren't you going downtown to see her school? And find her that way? What do you think you will need to be doing at night there? I'm really unclear on this."

"Okay."

"No, really. And I don't see why Mo and I can't try to get in touch with her before. Or why you can't. This all makes me very nervous. Very. To just catch someone unawares this way."

I got quiet. "I'm not trying to catch her," I had said.

Mom softened. "Of course not, darling. That's the wrong word. I just want to protect you. I want her to be ready to meet you! I want her to be her best self for you."

"I don't want her to run away again," I had said. "This will be okay, I just know it. I just want to see her. That's it."

Mom had hugged me then and then sort of pushed me away to look at me and then hugged me again, all cinema-style mom stuff.

"I just hope she wants to see you," Mo had said, also hugging me tight.

"Thanks a lot," I had said.

"Ivy," Mom had said. "You have to understand something. We just don't know her anymore."

"Hey, B," I say now to Patrick, shrugging it off, still. The memory and the worry. The past the present and the future, really, which is what we're kind of moving toward here. All at once. All at the same time. Just shrug it off, throw my bag in the trunk, keep my purse with all the stuff that we will need. Before I get in I lean into the window. "You brought snacks, right?"

Without snacks there is no road trip.

Patrick nods from inside the car and I open the door and pitch myself inside, set my bag down next to me: clothes for a few days, the rock, the letters. My evidence that I was once a person who was looked for.

I leave the locket at home, trapped with the spinning bal-lerina.

I watch my moms, still waving, try not to look at their sad, worried faces. I hook my head out and flash a big smile. "Bye!" I say, smiling more.

Then I duck back into the car, peer into the bag at my feet: gummy snakes, worms, bears, fish. I shake away that video everyone had posted about all the bones and muscles of teeny tiny helpless animals that go into our gummies. Just gross. Also: BBQ potato chips, tortilla chips. A tray of blondies.

"Where are the bagels?" I say?

"Dude," Patrick says. "Seriously? I made you blondies, dude."

I bump my head back. "Okay," I say. "Anyway, Claire will bring good stuff."

"Oh, really," he says, backing out of the driveway.

My moms. Still waving. The flash of Mo's silver rings.

"And what did you bring, princess?"

I smile and open my bag. "I have a bag of cheese sticks, an open bag of goldfish, and two yogurts."

"This? This is your offering? Your road trip fare?"

"I know," I say. "It was all I could do to get out of there. I had big plans for muffins but they were foiled."

I don't watch my parents watch me as they fade into the distance but I do wonder when they turn to go inside. And then Patrick has turned off our dirt road and onto asphalt, toward the highway.

I hit him on the shoulder. "Claire!" I say.

He rolls his eyes. "Must we?" He makes a big production of putting the car in reverse and turning the car around. Stick shift. I think the most romantic thing Patrick has done is teach me how to drive it. I am surprised the gears still work actually, as

I am sure, night after night in the high school lot I had to have stripped them down. I'm still not great on it. But, I don't know, I think it's nice to know how. I think it's cool.

We head over to Bridge Street to pick up our girl.

Claire sits on the front stoop: overalls, high-tops, hair down, all wavy-perfect.

"Ready?" I scream out.

"Ready," she says, standing.

I get out of the front seat and open the door for her faux gallantly.

"No way, you sit in front," she says, and then we faux fight.

"Hey, Claire," Patrick says when I push her in.

"Patrick." She nods, looking straight ahead.

I sit in the back, which is where I want to be, my head pressed up between them. "Hey, Mom, Hey, Dad!" I say. I feel like that. "When are we gonna get there?" I say, bobbing my head between them, pretending to be, like, four. I can do faux everything right now. But not sure how to do real.

They both turn and look at me.

"Ivy," they both say. "Where exactly are we going?"

A tray of blondies, a bag of gummy bears, a tub of Swedish fish, and two packages of lunch meat later, there are signs to the Palisades, and to bridges. I don't tell them about the registry site or the fact that I know where she might be. I don't tell them about the letter to the future I have in my bag, too, the only one I haven't read yet.

Boy Band again, just to make me insane I think. Signs to

bridges always means Manhattan is close, which I know from visiting Gram. Mom hates to go back to New York. Too much shit, she says. Outside or inside, I never ask. Like memories or just stuff to run into. Is it the past, her past, or does she mean the place, her place, or something I don't know yet? But there are bridges that lead us there. There is water to cross.

I sigh. Maybe it's the traffic Mom was referring to on every trip. Because no matter what bridge we have taken, I have never come into this city and not had to wait in a line to the moon to get in.

George Washington Bridge, says Boy Band. *Traffic ahead*, Boy Band says. *In nine miles, take the FDRrrr . . .*

This is where we turn off for Gram's. *Riiiight*, Boy Band says, and I ignore the voice, Claire's giggles, think of Gram with her pastel-colored macarons in waxy paper bags. Her soft leather flats on the pavement as we walked to the Met to see the Rembrandts, thick and sloppy with paint. Now *this* is a portrait, she'd said. Her long gloves. Her glasses on a golden chain.

"Here," I say. I point to her building. She's all the way east and we pull up in front and pause and we can all see across the river. There are a ton more buildings over there than there used to be.

The doorman knocks a knuckle on the window. I can see his double row of golden buttons sparkling, the metallic threads entwined in the ribbon shot through with light at the brow of his wool cap.

Patrick rolls down the window. "We're here—"

"To see Mrs. Cohen?" He smiles. He's always so sweet to me.

"Hello, Miss Ivy!" he says, smiling.

"Milton," I say, suddenly shy. "Hello." It's been a few years but one time we stayed here when I was a little girl, maybe eight, and Gram was having some kind of surgery. I played here in the lobby with Milton all afternoon long. He brought me checkers and Christmas crackers and all kinds of hard candies. I heard Mo ask if my grandmother was paying him and Mom got pissed off about it but they were both so uptight that visit—it was Mo who had made us come. After that, Mom said, she can visit us upstate if she wants to see us. I just can't, Mom said.

And she does, Gram, she comes and stays, makes a big fuss with her packages all tied up with fancy ribbons and strings, her spun-sugar desserts, her elaborate pillboxes and perfumes. It's like she's bringing the very essence of this place to us.

So Milton—he's been here forever. He has one of those faces that seems to spread out more over the years. His hair has always been white but now it's like a brighter white, escaping beneath that cap.

"Out, kids," Milton says. "Gimme those keys, my boy," he says to Patrick.

Patrick goes all splotched red. He hands the keys over in a way that makes me realize Patrick has never given the keys to anyone before. Like, he's never gone to dinner and had his car parked. It's weird that I have. That's all the stuff from my mom's past—the stuff she chose to leave behind. Was it a choice? I mean, did she *have* to in a way? Didn't she?

Milton takes our keys and who knows what he's doing with

Patrick's car but he guides me by the shoulder to the elevator. Here's the thing about New York City apartment buildings. They have these lobbies. Correction: the ones near Gram. Her friends. These ladies uptown. Golden and glass, fake flowers, brass. They are these old grand things and then step into the elevator and when you step out there is this brown carpet and old faded wall-paper and all darkness, no windows, a frightening hotel. Today it doesn't have the smell of old people food—cabbage and eggs and beets—but more of maybe dried roses. That's what Gram smells like, too, her rosewater, when she answers the door on the corner apartment, number 759.

Gram.

Gram!

Gram.

"Hi, Gram," I say. We all bow our heads and go inside.

"Gram, this is Patrick," I say.

He sticks out his hand and awkwardly says hello. I watch his hand come out of his jean jacket and it looks so weird, like it's not part of him, and then there's all this random, I don't know, guy hair, sprouting from his wrist. I don't love it.

"And you know Claire, right?" I say. "Remember her?" Claire has been around for years. We've been in school together since kindergarten.

She places her hand on the side of Claire's blond curls and says, "Darling, of course I remember her," right in her face.

"Come, darlings," she says, her pink lipsticked lips moving. "Sit down here."

Claire throws down her tote bag and her books spill out. The huge photo books. Some vintage fashion photography magazines. And that little paperback of New York orphans she got on road trip number one.

Gram ignores the spill of books and motions us grandly to a light blue couch—it's like silk or something—in front of the windows, heavy with curtains. I don't know why but I keep hearing the word "brocade" in my head when I look at them. There are big-paned windows and I pull my leg up beneath me and turn to the side so I can see out to the river, far below.

Tea sandwiches are laid out on a silver platter, I kid you not. I pick one up: cream cheese and cucumber and some kind of salad green, watercress, I think, as I pop it in my mouth. Then another, this one with some sort of brown spread. Pop that in, oh God, not into it at all.

Gram must see my face because she says, "Liverwurst, my dear, you need to learn to love it as I do, as I have."

Claire downs one. "Takes like Spam," she says.

"Spam?" Gram puts a hand over her heart, alarmed. "My lord no."

Claire just shrugs.

I grab a napkin from the fan of blue napkins next to the tray and bring it to my lips, spit out the brown sandwich, watch Patrick trying not to laugh.

"Now, Ivy, dear." Gram takes a swill off her drink. "Tell me what on earth you're doing with this *idea* you're having."

I snap to because this is only something I've heard about, from Mom. Like, I can't believe Gram is going to not just be nutjob leather and dessert-bearing Gram. But I am not into it.

"What's that supposed to mean?" I ask.

Claire clears her throat and Patrick scoots a little closer to me on this couch that is surely 112 years old.

"This notion that you want to find this 'other' mother of yours." She uses her fingers to make quotation marks. "Why bother?" Now she sort of waves her hand in the air. "What of it? Why do it is all. We all know Andrea is your mummy, and she has raised you after all, hasn't she, and why cause anyone more pain?" She nods her head. "I'm sorry I just don't understand the point in it."

This is the part where I can't believe this person is sitting across from me and I have never known this part about her, that she thinks finding the woman *who gave birth* to me is, like, a throwaway thing, that Gram, Gram!, doesn't understand, well, anything. Also? Mo is my mother, too. I was raised to respect my grandmother, all old people, really—Mo's mom is in Atlanta and she is awesome—but I can't really wrap my head around what is going down.

Claire slides in. "Well, it's important to Ivy, you know. There are so many unanswered questions after all."

Patrick nods. "I mean, I don't have those kinds of questions, and I imagine you don't. But Ivy wants very much just to see her."

My friends. I love them love them I do I do.

"Oh, sure, sure, I have many questions, believe you me, about all sorts of things. I mean, my mother was about as pure as the driven snow if you must know, I've got some questions there, and I've had my own life, too, if you must know, but *why* is my point, dear. Why. Let it *be*. Isn't your life good now, Ivy, darling? It seems rather charmed to me. Other than living in the sticks like a *farmer* as you do, by *choice*, well, it seems rightly charmed."

"Oh, does it?" I say. Is my life charmed? What does that even mean, really?

"When I think of what your mother went through to get you, well, I just can't bear it to be honest. What she did to have you."

"Gram. She didn't have me. I mean, she took me."

"Took? Hardly. And I'll tell you I have the bills to prove it."

I feel like I've been hit in the stomach with a two-by-four. I think Patrick's eyes are going to bulge out of his head. His parents don't comb their hair. They make a lot of stuff from hemp. They cook mostly ancient grains. I don't think he has ever witnessed about 1,001 things that are happening right now. I swallow, hard.

"So she bought me, then. Or you did."

Gram smiles. "No. My goodness no. I didn't mean that, Ivy." She shakes her head, cool as a cucumber. "Lovely shirt, by the way," she says, fingering my striped button-down. That and my wide-leg jeans feel about as cool as I get.

"So what did you mean then?" I ask.

Gram's blue eyes are blurry. She places her hand on my knee and I feel my body tighten. She is suddenly different to me. I don't want her to touch me.

"I want to protect you," she says. "I want things to stay as they are. With our family. My only grandchild. You. I want things to be just like this." She holds her arms out to the sky behind her. "I don't want it to change."

I am starting to doubt that I am the one everyone wants to protect here.

"It's not going to change. If I get an answer or see a face or meet a person. It's not going to change. I might change but I'm entitled."

Gram puts on a pouty face. "You might love me less. Maybe you won't want your old gram anymore. Maybe there will be another grandmother out there with all kinds of presents and kisses waiting for you. What will I do then, darling? You're my only."

"Only?"

"I'm counting on it!"

I roll my eyes. Now I am going to have to reassure my eighty-year-old grandmother, who is as mature as a ten-year-old. Tops. "I'll always love you, Gram," I say dutifully, though now I start to doubt it. Just at the edges. I go to hug her and I can see Claire on the other side of her. I roll my eyes her way now as I pat Gram's back.

"There, there," I say, imitating a grown-up. "Okay?" I pull away and look at my grandmother at arm's distance.

She wipes away a tear. I'm surprised at first and then strangely I expect it to be some kind of alien blue, like her eyes, like the sky, like the couch and the carpet, the napkins. All blue. But it's just a regular colorless tear. "Darling," she says, rubbing her hands along my arms now. "When did you get so grown-up?"

I smile. But even I can tell it's a different one than the smile I wore walking in here.

We finish up the tea sandwiches—well, the cucumber

ones—down some seltzers, and, yes, pop a purple macaron each down our gullets, and then we slap our thighs and tell Gram we're heading out.

"So soon?" she says, but I can tell she knows it's not soon enough for us.

I tell her we'll be back by eleven, a random number and I'm counting on her and my mother not having discussed, well, anything, but I want time. For what? Who knows. I don't. For the world to open up and swallow me or hug me or kick me to the moon. But here is this city that everyone has something to say about. Here is this city where my first mom lives.

"Good luck, Ivy," Gram says, all earnest and serious. "I love you, my dear," she says.

I smile back at her, genuinely, I love her, too, after all. I lean down and pick up Claire's books, place them on the side table in the vestibule. I open the door. Who knows what New York will bring us. Who knows? I think as I lead us down the old hallway, my fingertips skimming the walls, skipping to the elevator and down into the lobby, nod to Milton, and then out into the city, Manhattan, where I know, this time, all my answers lie.

NELLY HELLMAN

1955
Cornell University

Helen Farber looks at her friend in disbelief. The snow is blowing in wild bursts, as if by a leaf blower across the empty campus. Lake effect is not to be taken lightly. The snow is piling up in huge heaps. Which means getting to class—they each have a final exam in the morning—will be even more difficult tomorrow.

"Are you sure?" Helen asks.

Nelly shakes her head. "I'm sure, Helen. I've skipped two periods. I assure you."

Helen looks out onto the quad at the blowing snow. "Are you going to tell Harry?"

"Harry? My heavens, no!" Nelly says. "I can't. Honestly, I don't think he even understands one can get pregnant from such things. It was hardly even worth it. My goodness. Harry Cohen. My father would die for a hundred and three reasons. What will I do?"

They both turn to the window. All the snow. A blizzard, nearly.

"This is what we do. We take our exams tomorrow, as planned. Then we tell Abigail, because she has a car, and as soon as the streets are cleared we find a doctor."

Nelly looks up at the ceiling. She pictures Harry's sweet open face. His big smile. All that hair. His tennis rackets and sweater-vests. The thing about Harry is he would be a very good father. And he was kind in his way. But Harry was not who her parents were counting on, really. It was simply not the time. Not for her. And not for them. Nelly thought of the ridiculous class she was supposed to take: Homemaking Apartments 300, where two instructors, five students, and a baby (recruited from a local orphanage) live together in an appointed apartment for nearly two months. She'd even rejected the *course*. No thank you—her final tomorrow was in engineering. She was one of only two girls in that class.

"Okay," Nelly says to her roommate, relieved. "Thank you, Helen."

Helen goes over and pats her friend on the back and sits down across from her. "Let's put it out of our heads and get some sleep and then worry about it after the morning. Okay?"

Nelly climbs into her bed, her silk pillowcase cold and slippery beneath her face. It did keep the curls intact, though, much longer than her cotton cases. Helen turns off the light and in a short time Nelly can hear the sound of Helen's steady breathing. She thinks of telling Harry and maybe leaving school and perhaps going off with him and, well, being his wife, Homemaking Apartments in real life, and then someone's mother, to boot. Imagine. Someone's mother. It's what she wants one day, for certain, perhaps it was just a sooner moment than she'd anticipated. And then she thinks of that Homemaking Apartments 300 course. Of that motherless baby in the clumsy shaking hands of students. It feels wrong to her. So deeply wrong, but before she can think why it bothers her so, she is fast asleep until her alarm wakes her at 7:00 for this terrible day awaiting her.

Abigail Stoakly is a terrible driver in the snow. They slide across the street just getting out onto 79. They have three addresses but only one of the doctors is in town, the only one who will possibly perform an abortion. That one turns them away and sends them to Syracuse. After three hours, and two more doctors, they finally find someone—a friend of a friend of a cousin—who will do it but who wants more money than any of them has access to.

"We're going to be found out." Abigail white-knuckles the steering wheel of her father's Chrysler. "We'll be found out and arrested and you, Nelly, will have your baby in prison! We might all go to prison, don't you think?"

"Stop it, Abigail. I hardly think that helps," Helen says.

"Well, you two walk around like you're the bee's knees just leaving Sage Hall at any hour, doing as you please, and now look at you. Look at her."

Nelly is horrified. Mostly because Abigail is not wrong. For the first time her heart catches and she feels she will cry.

"Stop being such a bitch, Abigail," Helen says.

"Excuse me? How about you hitch home, then?" Abigail continues to drive, the car wobbling along in the snow. It's eerie and isolated on these streets.

"Stop, you two. Just stop it. Thank you, Abigail, for doing this. And, Helen, thank you for defending my honor and all of it. But maybe this is a sign. Maybe this isn't meant to be. Let's go back to school."

They both turn to look at Nelly in the back seat. "What are you saying, Nell?" Helen asks.

"Well, let's just say we do find someone. Not today or tomorrow, but sometime before my time is up and I pay him all the money he requires and I go in there alone and you, sweet friends, wait for me in some coffee shop nearby, and then what?"

"Then it's done," Helen says very calmly. "We pick you up and go back to school. Then it's over. It will be like it never even happened, Nelly!"

"But it isn't. You saw the papers. That girl in Albany died. She bled to death!"

"That was awful," Abigail said.

"That was one person."

"One girl," Abigail says.

"It isn't, though. There are all kinds of stories. And then there are the ones where the doctor reports you and then while you are almost bleeding to death you get arrested on top of it."

"Can you imagine?" Helen turns around. "Where are we anyway?" The snow is plowed but blowing madly around them, in massive swirls. It's as if for this moment they are the only people on the road, in this town, on this planet.

"I can't," Nelly says. "I can't do it. I'm not a rebel. It's just not who I am. I'm too scared. I'm not James Dean."

"Indeed," says Abigail, laughing. She had been so scandalized by that movie when she'd seen it in town the previous month. "I don't think he could be in your condition, now could he?"

Nelly leans back miserably. "Please, Abigail, just take me home."

"Home?"

"Back," Nelly says. "Just back."

Nelly is back at school the following fall, and in the end, it is in fact like none of it happens. She merely takes the spring off to be with her ailing father. It's a coincidence then, that he in fact does die, of heart failure. As if she's willed it. It's that September. Of course, she has not wished her father to be dead, but if it were to happen, which it was, his time was up, then this was as good a time as any. Nelly knows this is a horrible thing to think but she can't unthink it.

People know different sets of information, depending on the needs of the situation. Her mother knows what has happened and visits her daughter weekly at the Home for Unwed Mothers in Montclair. Her father, before he is taken gravely ill, believes his daughter is in summer school, at Cornell, safely installed. She comes to him in the hospital at an appropriate time, given the new semester of the school year, after she has given birth. Abigail and Helen know why she's gone, of course, and they receive her with knowing glances when she returns.

No one but Nelly Hellman knows, however, where the baby goes.

It is the one thing she insists on as she is being shuttled around and controlled and concealed, a punishment for two nights in bed with Harry Cohen, a wan lover at best. The baby—a daughter—goes to Susquehanna Valley, in Binghamton, New

York. Helen learns this, too, when she interrogates Nelly, who leaves each weekend for Binghamton to visit her. There, Nelly holds her daughter and feeds her a bottle. *Lulu Lulu Lu*, she calls her, it just feels like who she is, and then Nelly leaves to finish her studies and dance the twist and go to mixers and sneak brownies into the library and smoke cigarettes in the stairwell.

And then, one weekend in mid-February when she goes for her visit, her daughter is gone.

"Darling, did you think she'd be there forever?" Helen cradles Nelly, as she would a baby, she supposes, in her lap as her roommate weeps and weeps.

"Perhaps," Nelly sobs. "Perhaps I did. Yes, I did."

"But she needs a home, too," Helen says.

Nelly has fantasies of Homemakers Apartment 300—living with her own daughter for course credit. And an unrelenting fear that someone else is doing the same, someone she knows, perhaps. She wonders about everything: who her new parents are, what they look like, where they live, what their dreams are. Her name. How she wishes she had found a doctor that night and he had killed her with a dirty coat hanger. Surely, she thinks, that would have been easier. Than this.

What is her name?

But here Nelly is. And Harry. He has been so good. She broke it off with him, of course, but then, when her father died, he reappeared. He was there. He is a good man and perhaps they will have a future together. There is no need for him to know anything about it. What would he think? There is no one now to disapprove of Harry anymore, is there? Her mother isn't what they call *available* any longer. She is out from her gin by 8:00 p.m. Heaven knows Nelly is in no mood to be looking anymore. What would she find? Familiarity is a good, nice thing. And Harry is going to law school in the city, at Columbia.

The baby is gone, Nelly thinks as her dear friend smooths her hair out of her warm, wet face. Gone!

She can't stop imagining it. A big, open house with a grand staircase. A farmhouse, filled with animals and pies cooling on the sill. A room in a broken-down city. Lulu Lulu Lu. What do you do with all this wondering? Lulu.

"There, there," says Helen.

But she can't be soothed. Not really. Where is my baby?

She wonders will she ever have another thought again.

IVY

2017
New York City

Milton hails us a taxi to go downtown. I watch him hold out his hand, white gloved, and one just pulls up, smooth as Gram's silk couch.

It's this beautiful day. Golden light off the river, the cars, the building, casting all kinds of magic light.

We slide in, Patrick, me, Claire. The cabdriver says, "Where to, guys?"

Claire and Patrick look at me. "Yes," Claire says. "Wherever to?"

"You are being strangely enigmatic," Patrick says, squeezing my hand.

I unfold the printout that has been crumpled in my bag, smooth it out on the tabletop of my legs. "New York University," I say to the driver.

Claire looks over my shoulder, tilts her head. "What is that?"

The printout of the email. What the real one I didn't show my mothers says is: *Hi, Andrea. It's so nice to hear from you. I'm in school at NYU. Finally, school. And I'm in the classroom three days a week now. Teaching! I'm going to be a teacher. Hopefully. It would be great to see you and meet Ivy whenever she is ready.*

I never responded.

I lied to all of my mothers. And to this one I said I was searching on behalf of my mother, the adoptive one.

Because I didn't want to lie and tell her, yes, my parents know.

Because I got what I needed. New York City. Just as Mom thought.

Because what would I say?

"Yeah, what is that?" Patrick asks.

"That's a big place, my friend," our driver says, pretty much answering for me. "What building? Where? My niece goes there, I'm proud to say. Right on the beautiful Washington Square Park. But it's a big place. You can get very lost there."

"Washington Square Park!" I say to the driver. "We'll start there," I say to Patrick and Claire.

The driver turns off and we're on a highway along the river. Sailing beneath buildings and through tunnels and down down down until he turns off and cuts into the city. There's something so exciting and so terrifying about being here, on our own. Forget what I am looking for. Being here, the three of us, just having a day in this place, all our own.

The driver pulls up to a street corner. "There," he says, pointing.

What do I see? Paths to a fountain, catching golden light. It's after three already, we're, like, starting out in the evening, and here is an arch in the distance, casting shadows. It feels like I'm already too late as I pay and we get out, hands in pockets that somehow makes it seem like we know what we are doing or where we are supposed to be going.

We get out of the cab and Claire says, "Please say you know where you're going."

"I gotta say," says Patrick, "I'm with Claire on this one. Where we going, B? Is she even here? In New York? We just sort of let you lead us without really asking very much because this is your thing," he says.

Claire nods.

I look at my friend and my boyfriend, in agreement on something for maybe the first time. I take I deep breath.

I nod. "Yes," I say. "She's here. She's at school here." I point to a building that I now see is the library.

"Tell me," he says.

"Yes, tell us." Claire hits Patrick on the shoulder.

Then I do it. I explain how I contacted her by saying I was my adoptive mother and that she is somewhere in this city taking classes, probably NYU.

"Probably?" Patrick says.

"No, she said it. Okay, look." I pull out the printed note and unfold it, like it's a map to something, which in a way it is.

Claire takes it. She reads and nods.

"She does say NYU." She hands it to Patrick.

He reads it, too.

"Okay," he says. "So we can assume she does classes when she's not teaching, and if she teaches three days a week, I mean, who does stuff Monday, Wednesday, and Thursday, right?"

I am eager to be helped and my eager nodding reveals this.

"So tomorrow is Friday. Where does she teach?"

I shrug. Claire throws up her arms.

"Okay, then," Patrick says. "Or we could look for her around here but, I mean, how will we do that?"

Claire is on her phone and she holds it up to us. There is a teeny tiny map of the campus, like a map to a dollhouse compound. "The teaching school is over there." She points to the section of the park where we were dropped off. "We could see if we can get any info from the office there."

"We could!" I say. I feel hopeful.

"We could," Patrick says. "I'm sure they wouldn't mind, like, giving all kinds of information about a student. I'm sure that won't be a problem."

The day. The day! It is shining and music is playing and it smells like pretzels and salt and weed and spring. I kind of just want to be in this day, too. "Should we pretend we're someone?" I ask.

"Pretend?" Claire says incredulously.

"You're her *daughter*," Patrick says, and I feel like I will throw up.

"Let's go," Claire says. "This is why we're here." She pulls me by the wrist, Patrick following, as we go across the park and out and into the building across the street with the NYU purple flag flying.

We enter the building and, before we can even get our breath, we are stopped immediately.

"ID, please," the man at security says, pointing at the high-tech walk-through machines that have winded us when they stopped so suddenly as we tried to pass through.

"Oh, sorry, we don't have one. I'm actually, well"—I look

around the steel lobby—"I'm actually looking for my mother?"

"Really, now," he says, crossing his arms. His badge shines. He widens his stance.

"No, really, she is," Patrick says.

"You all students here?" he asks.

We all shake our heads. No.

"Call your mother and tell her to come get you."

"The thing is," I say, "I don't have her number. I mean, she's not expecting me. She doesn't know me."

There is some heavy nodding, from everyone now.

"Well, no ID, no entry," he says.

"Awww, really?" Claire says. "We came all this way."

"Honey," he begins, and I see her bracing. "This is New York City. We have to be strict about who comes in here. There is a lot of stuff that goes down around here you don't want to know about. You look like very nice kids and I hope you find your mother, but you can't come in this building or any other NYU building without ID."

Patrick salutes him. "Got it," he says.

And we turn and walk out of the building and into the sun.

What is the opposite of hopeful? I suppose that's easy: it's hopeless. I suppose that is what I feel then. Utterly. Patrick senses this and he takes my hand.

"We're locked out of all the buildings," I say.

"Now would probably not be the time to say you might have planned this a bit better?" Claire says.

"Claire," says Patrick.

"No, she's right," I sort of groan. "I don't know what I was thinking. I mean, how big can NYU be?"

We all start laughing. It's, like, bigger than our town.

We walk back into the park, toward the center, the fountain area, and all these people are just, like, hanging out. Hippies and punks and kids and old people and musicians and magicians and guitars and keyboards, dogs, cats, a parakeet, children screeching. A policeman is ticketing a guy playing the piano.

"D'oh!" Patrick says, as if that's how the boyz in the city tawk.

"Stop it," I say. I know he's been so helpful and supportive, but there is one thing I know: I am just always myself. Whoever that is? It is always me. Please, I think, Patrick, just stay you.

We sit down on a bench looking out at the fountain, buildings of the university behind the sprays of water and puppies and screaming people.

"Man, this is a tough place. No entry. Also ticketing a street performer. Nice, friendly town." Patrick has his hands in his jacket pockets, like two guns pointing at the police guy who hands the piano player a ticket. He has a real piano.

"Where is she?" I say. "I really wonder now."

"I just assumed you *knew* where she was," Claire says.

"Claire!" Patrick says.

"I'm sorry but we came down to do this! I am having a good time and everything but can we not forget we did come down here for a reason."

I don't say anything. I am realizing as they're talking how much I want to meet her and just see her face and who she is so that I can also be me. It's everything. That is, anyway, what it feels like today. I know I messed up. I know that this time I can only blame myself for thinking the world will just gather in around me and, I don't know, do its thing. Reveal itself. I know, somewhere in here, that it isn't everything, too, as in, other things get to happen. In my life. And who knows, maybe in hers, too. In hers, too.

I wonder.

"Do you have anything else?" He follows my gaze until I am looking him in the eye.

I dodge it just the same. "I don't know," I say.

"Like where she teaches, say?" Claire asks.

I just look down. I wriggle my toes but of course they can't see that.

"Okay," Patrick says, breathing. "How long did it take her to write Pretend Andrea back? When you wrote her on the site?"

"Like twenty-four hours?" I say. "Maybe less. It was really surreal. Like maybe she wants to be in touch."

"Okay, let's just go back on to the site and ask her where she is. Like in an unthreatening Andrea kind of way. Man, this is just so unethical, Ivy."

"Like what's your day like? That kind of a thing."

"Unethically, yes," Patrick says.

"Unethical? I mean, I can't go on the site until I'm eighteen. And I didn't want to get my moms involved. And I think I have a right. Ethical?"

"Okay. She's kind of right," Claire says. "She does have a right."

I take my phone out and log in. I start to type a message,

but then I'm stuck. Utterly. What do I write? Her last message had said: *I am in school now, finally.* What do I say? That's fantastic and can I get the address and class times? In case I want to stalk you?

I hand the phone to Patrick. "You," I say.

Patrick types something. His swiftness is shocking and kind of, umm, thrilling. "Okay?" He turns the phone toward me. *That is wonderful to hear, Bridget. Where are you student teaching? I used to live in New York, remember?!? Best of luck to you.*

"Okay," I say, because that is exactly what my mom would say, and, again without hesitation, I hear the swoosh of him sending it.

Nothing to do but wait now, I think. I look at Patrick and Claire. I shield my eyes from the sun.

"Now what?" I say.

What we do is walk toward that ticketed piano, silent now, and there's a dog park over there, too, all the bizarre city dogs in one teeny space, the smell of pee and poop and sawdust. Big dogs on one side, little ones on the other, yipping and yapping, barking.

I miss Court and Spark.

A group of kids sits on the benches by the dog park. Old-school boom box, splattered with paint. On purpose? All different kinds of boys. One's got a feather in his hair, dancing, one's got an Afro with a comb still stuck inside it. Our life? Me and Claire and Patrick? Whiteville. This is like, all the stuff. The boy with the feather dances on the seat, dogs yapping behind him: *Wreckin' shop, when I drop these lyrics that'll make you call the cops,* goes the music but I've got no idea who's singing it.

I think we're all staring. At everything but also at these three boys because they are our age. I can just tell, the way I can tell when a dress I see online will be perfect on me. I can see it and feel it and know it to be true. Now a girl turns the corner, all decked out, Goth: black ripped tights, black Docs, black kohl, blue-black hair, white white skin but it's powder; you can't tell her color underneath. She's not really having any of it from these boys.

"Stop," she says. "I'm going home soon, just cool yer jets," she says. She doesn't smile but there is a smile in there anyway.

There is this crazy golden afternoon light. Spring light, though, so it's white, too. It's wonderful. It's all so transfixing.

"What up?" says one of these boys to the others.

"Baruch atah Adonai Chelsea Ping-Pong at the Twins' or BK with Jonathan?"

Then one of those boys looks over at us. "What up, kidz? You need somefin'?"

We laugh nervously.

"Where you from there, children?"

Claire, the fearless, says, "Upstate."

"Ha," one of the boys says. "Not bridge and tunnel as suspected. Just full-on tourists. Full-fledged foreign."

"Funny," says Patrick. I know it's killing him. He loves to be the cool one, and where we are, he usually is. Unless Alex is there. Alex trumps all. Somehow, though, Patrick fits in everywhere.

"We're on this kind of mission," Claire says, like, totally trading in my story for love and respect.

"Yeah?" Cocked head.

The girl looks up, curious.

"Hmmm," Patrick says, sensing approval.

They look at me but I'm not going to say anything. These people are strangers.

"Her birth mom lives here." Claire points at me, like, outing me.

"Got it."

"She's looking for her, I mean. Ivy is. She's never met her."

The kid with the giant 'fro comes forward. "Really?" he says.

I nod. "Yup. I'm from adoptionland, really." So I guess I say something.

Everyone sort of snaps to. Hello, they seem to be saying. Funny person gets the hello. Always.

"I'm adopted," the guy who has approached us says.

Patrick, excited, says, "That's so cool. From where? Ethiopia?"

"'Scuse me, man?"

"What?" Patrick asks, already turning red.

"Patrick!" I say. It comes out like a gasp. He has just undone the handsomeness of sending that email. I can see Claire shaking her head, her eyes closed.

"My first mom is in New Jersey. What are you talking about, brother?"

Splotchy red Patrick nods. "Sorry, man. So sorry."

"He knows," I say.

"Knows what?" says Patrick through his embarrassment.

"Well, that not all black children are from Africa, for one," I say. "Adopted ones or bio kids."

Patrick nods. "I do know that," he says. "I so know that. God, I'm so sorry."

He nods. "Yeah, well, she's in Jersey," he says, just to me. "I've met her, but it's not that pretty anymore."

This alarms me and my heart rate speeds up. But I play it cool, shrug. "Who knows," I say. "Don't even know if she's here. I think she's at NYU." I nod vaguely behind me to the building we were just in. "They won't let us in without any ID to try to find her."

"Right on," says the light-skinned boy. He's got black hair, combed close to his head, shined and flattened with some sort of pomade and kind of a 'stache but more like trying.

"Jonathan," the adopted one says. The adopted one. I can't imagine if someone referred to me this way. I'd slice her in half.

Jonathan goes to shake my hand. Long, bony fingers. I shake this hand. Then Claire, then Patrick, clearly still mortified that he thought this kid was from Ethiopia and that he actually said it, too.

"Can't unknow her once you know her. All's I'm saying. She expecting you?"

I shake my head, think of her believing she was writing to my mother. I can switch it up, too, am I right? I get to choose, too, okay? NYU, she wrote back. Finally I'm in school, finally I'm in the city.

Well, I got some power, too.

The boy with the boom box, covered in paint, twirls over. "Avi," he says, waving.

We wave back.

"And this"—he curtsies—"is Andre."

Andre wiggles his fingers.

"And Tina? Don't even bother with her. She's here because we've been in school together forever. Otherwise? Where would you be otherwise, T?"

Tina says to the ground. "Anywhere." She looks up briefly. "Else."

"Okay, so let's go hang out at my place in Brooklyn," Jonathan says to his friends.

"So that's the decision?" Pomade says.

Jonathan nods. He is so clearly the Alex of the bunch here.

Patrick nods.

Jonathan looks at him, shakes his head. "You guys can come if you want."

He slings his backpack over his shoulder, Pied Piper–style.

"We're waiting on a message from the birth mom," Claire says.

I give her the stink eye. But then I realize: he's the Alex, so he's got Claire's attention. "I messed up, okay? Anyway, it looks like we'll be looking for her tomorrow."

Tina rolls her eyes.

"Totally!" Patrick says, so eager, so embarrassing. I can't tell if it's because he believes he's been forgiven or if it's because he wants some kind of adventure.

We all do. We all want both those things.

You can't unknow her, I hear this Alpha Jonathan tell me again and again like some kinda movie voice-over.

Claire smiles in her kitten way. "Yes," she says. "Okay, Ivy?"

Gee, thanks for checking in, best friend. But I get it. It's all an experience. Our New York day. Who will we tell when we return to school? And how would we say no? What would that make us? Losers is what. Tourists is all.

"Here's what we do. We go eat us some wasabi Belgian fries and then we hop on the F train and we go to Jonathan's place."

"Why are you acting all too cool for school?" Tina asks them, hopping off her bench. Then, moving her head side to side, she mimics, "We're going to eat some fries and go to J's, like we do. It's not all hop the F train shit, aight. Don't freak out the foreigners. And also? Hate that wasabi sauce."

"Umm, we're not foreigners," Patrick says again.

They all look at him, death stare. But Patrick is right—it's not so different from how we hang out. I mean, it's just the setting is changed. The background.

"Really," Avi says.

Patrick shrugs. "Not that foreigners are bad or anything. We're just not. Foreigners," he says. "Just saying. But foreigners—and immigrants and refugees—are cool."

Everyone looks at Patrick. Everyone cracks a smile. "And migrants?" says Jonathan.

"Totally," he says, not realizing there's a joke at his expense.

And then the joke is over and it's true. We're all the same, I want to say, but I don't say it. I don't say anything at all.

They all start moving, even Tina and what the hell, *dang* if we don't follow, *dang* if we don't all get extra-large fries with curry ketchup and then go down into the subway, down again, deep below, humid, hot, smell of pizza and stale beer and sweat, board the F train, hold on tight, feel like we're in this *gang*, like this New York kid gang and then we get off a few stops into Brooklyn and out we come, shock of the end of a sunny day, streets lined with town houses (brownstones, we are corrected), little kids screaming in a park, legs pumping on their kid swings, dogs on leashes, wagging tails, like this urban suburban paradise, this Brooklyn. And then we are at an old brick building, an ex–candy factory we are told, climbing up stairs and then key in the door and then we all file into this Jonathan person's apartment.

LULU

It is the second letter Lulu has received since she turned eighteen. She retrieves it from the mailbox at the end of the long, twisty driveway before her parents will have the chance to see it.

Indeed, the contents from the state are the same as they had been from the city. The records are closed. She will not be permitted to see her original birth certificate. She will never see the name of the woman who gave birth to her next to her own. She will likely never even know that woman's name.

But often she imagines her, and her birth father as well. As she watches her own mother pouring cream-of-chicken soup onto noodles and adding tuna—every Tuesday night!—Lulu imagines her mother, the real one, is Joni Mitchell. The song "Little Green" torments her: *You're sad and you're sorry but you're not ashamed. Little green have a happy ending.* She listens to the album, *Blue,* over and over and over, the grooves on the record scratched from use on this song. She imagines that it could be her. Canada, where the musician hails from, is not, after all, so far from this cold, hard place in Upstate New York. It is possible.

Lulu rips up the letter and throws it in the trash, takes out her box from under her bed, the one with her 45s (the Jackson 5,

Stevie Wonder, Janis Joplin, the Kinks, Aretha, the Beatles) and the letters from Ray, two George McGovern pins, even though her parents were both for Nixon, both of them!, and also a roach clip with a blue feather attached. She lights up and sucks at the very end of it, lies back in her bed, and does what she has done so often in this room, which is to think about the what ifs. The if onlys. Like regular ones: like, if only Ray hadn't gotten drafted. Would they still be together? Maybe. He'd be home, that's for sure. She wouldn't have to read his sad, desperate letters begging her to wait for him. She will wait, though. It's the least she can do, isn't it? And what else is there anyway here?

If only her dad had gotten a job in Boston or New York City or any city at all like he'd always said he would. Then they wouldn't be stuck here in this teeny town where everyone knows everyone's business. She wonders, for a moment, what it had to have been like for her parents when they brought her here. People, still, say the stupidest things.

Then her thoughts drift as they always do, to all the other things. Like who *were* they? The parents. Hers. Were they cool? Were they glamorous? Were they beautiful? Were they young? Old? Were they the same religion? Were they artists? Were they bankers or lawyers or candlestick makers? Did they like the beach, like she does? Did they climb trees and mountains and sail seas? Did they travel? Did they want to? Could they curl their tongues? Were they double jointed?

Could she whistle? Her birth mother. What is her name?

Lulu can't whistle. She can't curl her tongue, can't wink. Can't do anything but the usual stuff with her face, and she wonders if that isn't a genetic trait. If it means something.

Is she alive? Her birth mother.

Lulu knows she is alive. She knows if she were dead that she would feel it, somewhere, like in her *cells*.

She does this thing: She makes up her own mother. Her own father. The mother is in a sundress and she has dark straight hair, like Lulu has. She is always in this yellow dress even in winter. She is always tan and shining as all girls in yellow sundresses do. There is a father, too, but Lulu thinks of him less. It's her mother she pictures, her blue eyes, her freckles, the bones of her clavicle.

It's winter here. It just snows and snows. It's always snowing here. Everything hushed. *Swish swish* is the sound everyone makes in their parkas, their mittens against their faces, snow in their eyelashes and hair. It's late December but they've been bundled up for months. Snow covers their houses, the front lawns, the cars, trash cans. Snow: It covers everything but it also outlines it. In a way, it makes everything more clear.

We are all so far away from each other when it snows, Lulu thinks.

Soon it will be the new year, but what has changed?

Is Ray even alive? She wonders that, too, because he hasn't written in a week and that could mean anything. She would feel his passing, too, wouldn't she? There are so many different kinds of love, really, too many ways to feel it leaving you. But, Lulu believes, he is still out there and he will be back.

A new year. 1973: the past is blank and white and unreachable. She wonders about Ray in some rain forest, his boots filling with mud. It's like that, isn't it? Over there. But so is the future.

There is nothing out there that she can see. It's all emptiness and blackness.

And now? Here? In her bedroom in this house in this town in New York State, where she hangs out alone and sometimes with her friend Valerie whose boyfriend is also in Vietnam, she smokes her weed and listens to Janis and Joni. This is nothing, too.

This is 1973, thinks Lulu. I am eighteen years old. This is just the beginning.

Where did everybody go?

IVY

2017
Brooklyn

It's light in here at Jonathan's place, I'll say that, but it's teeny. Like, kitchen in one corner, a counter, facing a living room. Everything's got personality I guess. Lots of paintings on the walls. Black-and-white photographs of dancers. I go look at the photos on the mantel and there's Jonathan at all his ages, framed by two white people, a man and a woman. She's pretty—long hair, bangs that get longer as she gets older, light freckles splashed across her face, gifts from the sun, Gram calls them, pretty patterned dresses. Like what Claire might look like when she's older. And he's good-looking, too. A dimple in his chin, nice black hair, grayer and grayer as Jonathan gets older. Jonathan is cute as all get-out when he's a baby. You can tell they don't know what to do with his hair for a while, and then they do. And then he does. In every picture they are staring at him the same way my moms do: just all this love. Like, so much. Like, they know this is a gift they almost didn't get to open.

I know how that can feel, which is too much, like, overwhelming. Who wants to be a gift? You know what goes into being wrapped up in paper and pretty ribbons? Tall order because we have stuff inside, too, and it's not all gift-wrapped in fancy paper.

"They're in Arizona," says Jonathan, though no one has asked him. He goes to the fridge and pulls out a jug of OJ. Gets down some glasses. Kneels down and comes up with a big bottle of vodka, starts pouring. "My dad's got a show at a museum in Phoenix." *Glug glug* goes the vodka. "Lots of cactuses and fruit bats, judging from the pics they keep sending me. And ghosts, according to my mother, who says the car goes freezing and the lights go out on the dash in the same spot on some strange stretch of road they have to drive to the museum."

"Really?" Avi says.

"Guess so," Jonathan says.

Tina nods.

"They leave you alone here?" I ask. The amount of preparation it would take for my moms to leave me alone would be an enormous undertaking for us all. But New York–style, I guess.

"Naah. I'm supposed to be at a friend's." Jonathan is handing out drinks. He's so easy in his skin, like he could be a bartender for real. Or a kid in his parents' apartment. Both work for me right now.

"J's dad's a painter. Kind of well known," Tina says. "Andrew Laherty?"

I stare at her blankly.

"Well, I mean, like, in the art world. Art-world well known."

Art World? Not World world? These people talk like they are in magazines. Music World? Is that a thing? Also I realize then that Tina loves Jonathan. She probably knows everything about him. I wonder about these details now, like, is there a birthmark? A secret letter, like I have? A rock? I'm not sure he notices Tina much, but I remind myself to watch and see.

Claire sips at her drink now and I watch her watch him, too, just over the lip of her glass. The boy in charge.

This, I'm seeing, could get ugly.

Outside I can see a subway go by and it looks pasted against the sky. Also the tops of buildings, strange uneven shapes, fire escapes. It's totally soulful and beautiful.

Jonathan shrugs. "I guess," he says.

He's done passing drinks and I set mine down and look at my phone, think about getting back to Gram's.

Claire is flashing one of her sideways smiles and I realize we might be in this for a while, so I might as well just relax and let it all go down however it's going down. Maybe there is destiny in this, too. The original plan got derailed hours ago, so who knows what I'm meant to be doing tonight.

Patrick takes my hand. He weaves his fingers in mine, squeezes all our fingers. *Hi*, I think. *Hi*, Patrick. I look at him. He's all in, too. Always has been and tonight I like that. Tonight that doesn't feel like the whole wrapped-up-present thing, which it can feel like, all too much and all about opening me up to see what's inside, but tonight it just feels nice and strong and important.

So this is what happens at Jonathan's:

Claire starts drinking and so does that Avi and then he calls his friend who I think is his boyfriend and also he calls the Twins who are now the Twins of Ruth for some reason that has to do with custody and their parents recently divorcing and who live in Chelsea and apparently have a Ping-Pong table, as we'd heard, and then Tina looks up from her book and is like, I'm in this, too, and Andre goes home somewhere along the way and then this happens: Claire goes off with Jonathan. I watch her trail after him, as if she is a Squirmel and he has her on a magical Squirmel string. Off, into his room, and sure enough Tina starts drinking straight from the vodka bottle and then, here we go, she's crying hysterically, like for her whole life, which seems like it's been okay actually other than being the middle kid and not getting into the private school her sister got into, which I find out when I sit on the couch with her, holding her hand, and then Avi and his friend sit down, too, and we're all like talking about our most sad and private things to make Tina feel better, like how Avi once held hands with his friend, a boy, in the backseat of his mother's car when he was eight and she was driving in New Jersey and she turned around and screamed at him that boys don't marry each other and then they got in a car crash, right there and then, and so, as a result, Avi will always think of love as a car crash, because he loved this boy so much, he tells us, and Tina nods and says, whispering, I will always only love Jonathan and that is also like a car crash even if the blood is on the inside, and then she weeps and weeps and says she could die from this feeling, she knows it, and it's getting dark out now, the sun is setting wild with clouds and orange and pink and the room is filling up with darkness but no one moves to turn on a light, not yet, and Avi and his friend, who is Benjamin, hold hands and start kissing, and that's when the Twins of Ruth arrive, they get buzzed in and they are not identical, and they take a look and say, oh shit, this is some ugly going on in here, and then they pour themselves vodka and OJs, too, and they sit down on the rug and say, fill us in, and Patrick does and also nods to the room where Jonathan and Claire are, and then to Tina, and I don't know what to do because I want Claire to be okay and even though I don't know her I want Tina to feel better, too.

Is Claire okay in there? I mean, who is Jonathan, really? I can't ask Tina, but her love for him gives me hope that he is lovable and good and worthy of my friend's temporary affection.

I look around. Well, I know where he lives, there's that. Also, Claire is a big girl. I remember the first time she kissed Keith Summers in my backyard in seventh grade. That seemed so scandalous at the time, the way she had snuck off with the captain of the soccer team and then came back all smudged up. But why was it a scandal? What was the part that was scandalous I don't know now. Was it the leaving bit?

People are talking about food because there have only been french fries since being in the city, so there is talk of pizza and ordering it or going out for it and still there is no light, but Brooklyn is lit up now and the streetlights are coming into the dark room, and also stores across the street, other people's apartments and I can see a couple fighting right before me, in a building across the street, there are her hands on her hips and she is in her bra and underwear just screaming her head off. Is that love? In another apartment I can make out a woman, alone, rocking a crying baby to sleep.

It's like a dollhouse here/there and I look over at Jonathan's door and it's still closed and, man, I can see Tina is watching it like her eyes are shooting darts of ancient fire and I can tell she's all cried out.

"I'm going home," Tina says.

"You got a Lyft or want a car?" Avi asks her, sweetly, and this means a way home, because Tina lives in a different part of Brooklyn and no one seems to drive anywhere or have their parents pick them up or drop them off; it's like a whole other *system* here.

"Lame-o shame-o," say the Twins of Ruth. "We're going to Natalie's."

Apparently this is all the way back in Manhattan somewhere, though this doesn't seem to bother anyone, no one seems to worry about getting anywhere in fact.

"See ya, J!" they scream at Jonathan's closed door, and they leave and Tina goes out behind them, silently.

I creep back to the bedroom door and tap on it and say, "Claire?" *Tap tap.* "You in there?" *Tap.* "We have to leave soon."

I hear shuffling and then Claire says, "Let's stay a little longer, kk? All good here."

What can I say? And I can't tell if the kk is real.

And then Avi and Benjamin are like, "Should we make out here all night or go to a club?"

They decide on a club but then we all realize that it's not even 9:00 p.m., so we call for the pizza, bang on the bedroom door now, screw this delicate *tap tap*, for his address. Jonathan screams it out, muffled—gross—and then we order two pies, one with some form of meat and one with mushrooms, and then we wait and the boys drink more and even Patrick drinks some, too, me too actually, why the hell not?, and I think how am I going to get Claire out of here.

That's when Benjamin screams. Like curdle-the-blood scream.

"What?" I say, heart pounding. "What!"

"Mu-sic!" Avi and he say at the exact same time.

Avi runs over to a phone port he must know about and soon out blasts: *You're just a kid, but you got nowhere to go.*

They go insane dancing. Jumping on the couch.

There is a rumble in the streets of soul, they scream/sing.

It's loud and sort of awful and I just want to leave but what will we do? I am suddenly exhausted. Like paralyzation. I have been moving and moving and not stopping, not even in my mind, and now it's all, like, grinding to this incredible stop. I feel there is an extreme purposeless to my life now, to this mission I have been on, that brought us here, and it feels like even though it hasn't even begun, it's already over.

I just want to lie down. Alone. So I go to the door leading to the other bedroom and open the door.

It's just a bedroom that belongs to someone else's parents. Big bed, TV, some cool paintings, one with the name *Sally* painted in red and yellow brushstrokes across the canvas, and more photos, lots of papers stacked around. I flop down on the bed, watch Avi and Benjamin move in the living room. They're dancing, hard, and I can't tell if they're serious or not. Benjamin's frizzy blond hair bops by, flailing, and then there is Avi, all dark and contained, robotic almost, they're kind of opposite in that way I think. Are Patrick and I more the same?

Patrick comes in and stands at the door and, swear to God, just as he does it, someone turns on a light in the living room and he's silhouetted now, just this shape I want to lie down next to me, make me feel like it will all work out, like I will find her.

He walks in and closes the door behind him and he sits on the bed next to me the way my mother does when I am sick and she is brushing back my hair out of my face, but then it changes and we are kissing, like in the car that time after the road trip to Ithaca, just kissing like it will save us or kill us and it is really beautiful tonight in this dark.

For the first time I want everything with Patrick. To be with him completely, on this adventure, and maybe that's because he's with me tonight, I'm not with him, like at band practice, and maybe that's what I came for, to lose my virginity, maybe that's what Claire is doing next door to me right now, maybe it was *this* we were coming for and not to see my first mom because, as Jonathan concurs, that is something I cannot unsee. A thing I cannot unknow.

Maybe the butterfly wings flapping in South America made this happen tonight.

I am all in now.

And while losing my virginity cannot be unlost, I suppose, I want Patrick, and for the first time I am absolutely sure of it and I feel him so close to me. He brushes his fingers over my chest and moves back to unhook my bra, as he has countless times.

The feeling of the release of the clasp and also that he did it, with one hand, that he knows me and knows how, it just makes me want more and more of him and I reach for him, which I have done, but I don't usually do it first, and I brush my fingers over his jeans and I unhook his belt and I feel like I know him, too, like I did *that* to his belt, and I get the button of his cords undone, then his zipper.

We are kissing, hard, and I touch him. Because it can be my choice. I can have power, too. It feels natural and perfect and like I'm not thinking and then Patrick grabs my wrist, a little suddenly, and sort of harshly, which feels shocking.

"Stop." He stops kissing me and brings me to him.

I push back a bit, teasing I suppose, but also saying, yes, I said yes, I mean yes, did you not get that?, you have wanted this answer since you put that stupid pencil in my hair in English class, but he blocks me again.

"Ivy." He moves my hand. "Now's not the time."

I realize he's serious. "Why?" I say, sort of insulted, rejected, though I know he's into it, I mean, the bulge, it can't lie, can it? "Isn't this what you wanted?"

"Of course. My God, of course. It's not the right time. It's just not. Where are we? What are we doing? I mean, this is just not how I want it to be with you. I love you."

"I love you, too, and it feels right to me. That is all. It never has before really. I mean, I wanted to is all." I try to lessen the rejected-little-girl feeling I'm holding on to by just being honest. It's hard, though. Hard not to get mean and invulnerable.

"This needs to be the weekend you find Bridget," Patrick says.

He's done it. He's said her name. It, like, breaks some spell. It's all broken now. The sex spell, for sure, but also some other thing I can't put my finger on.

I sit up and turn on the bedside light. "Got it," I say, feeling the mask of me come back. I had liked the way it had dissolved—for a moment I was just me, just my face.

"Come here," he says, sitting across from me, cross-legged. He holds me awkwardly, then moves to button his pants and straightens himself up. So I fidget around and try to be cool and elegant as I redo my bra. It doesn't work at all. Not at all.

"You know," I say, "I might not ever feel this way again."

He looks at me sideways. "That would suck," he says.

"Just letting you know. That could have been your chance."

He scrunches his mouth into a sideways smile. "Ivy," he says.

I pretend-pout. I don't like it but I do. I cross my arms.

"Come here," Patrick says again. He's seated against the headboard, fully clothed.

I climb on top of him and wrap myself around him. Spider hug. "Fine," I say.

He brushes my hair back out of my face, exposing it, mask or no mask, I can't decide. "And it's our chance, you know that, right?" he says.

I'm silent.

"Now, can we just get Princess Claire out of her tower and get back to Gram's house before we turn into little mini city pumpkins."

"You're mixing up your fairy tales," I say, climbing off him.

Push my hair back over my face, over my eyes.

This whole thing is a mixed-up fairy tale, I think.

We stand and I open the door and Ben and Ari have stopped dancing. They have now descended upon the pizzas that must have shown up while we were in here. It's carnage—tomato sauce all over the white stools and white countertop. Crime scene–style. New York gangsters.

"Do you need any money?" Patrick asks as we pull off slices of mushroom and shove them into our mouths.

"Welcome to our country," Avi says, bowing. "New York pizza. On us."

Patrick nods and shoves a piece of mushroom into his mouth.

It's delicious. I am ravenous and I devour the piece and pull off another.

I look at Jonathan's door. "Any movement?" I ask the boys.

Benjamin shrugs. Then Avi does the same.

I put down my pizza and walk over to the door. "Claire?" I say, tapping lightly. "Honey?"

I hear shuffling and then the door opens. Claire. Fully clothed. Unscathed. Less smudged than when she kissed Keith Summers in the woods in my backyard.

"So soon?" She looks back at Jonathan who is equally clothed. On the bed there are about thirty black-and-white photos laid out. Several large portfolios are open, and drawings are scattered around the floor. I can see several charcoal drawings of Jonathan on the night table, one seated with his legs crossed, like mine, I can't help but note, one smoking a cigarette and looking out the window. There is a contour drawing of him standing, his arms outstretched, about to take flight. Just from his outline, he looks like Alex.

They sort of take my breath away. The pictures and the people. I remember looking at my friend drawing me. I wonder if he feels the same intensity of recognition that I did that day.

Found.

"All right, then!" is what I say. Then, "We have to go now," and we grab our jackets and hug and the boys do that chest-press thing, which annoys me because it's like more touching than a hug, so why not just hug?, and then I download a Lyft app and then we get one coming and then we are out the door down the stairs out on the street and then we are in someone's car and we are moving and Claire is saying, what an amazing person he is, he's so smart, and I loved *drawing* him, then we are on the Brooklyn Bridge and I am looking out at all the other bridges, the line of them connecting us, these steel promises that we won't float away, and then we are flying uptown and then we are at Gram's, finally, pulling up, and Claire grabs my shoulder, whispers in my ear, "I want to *be* Alex," she says. "That's the answer."

I look over at my friend. "You are," I say. "But you're Claire." I yank a little at her sleeve to make sure she knows that.

And then I thank the driver and I don't know this doorman who opens the door for us but he knows me, and we are in the weirdo, hideous, glamorous dusty old lobby, empty now, still as a funeral parlor, and we are in the elevator and out on the dark, smelly hallway, tonight it's like Vick's VapoRub and cabbage, and then, here we are, here we are at Gram's apartment.

I take a big breath. I ring the bell. It's 10:55 and we made it and we are chewing our gum and Gram, expecting us because of course the doorman called up, opens the door in her blue silk robe and her pink lipstick and she says, "Oh, darling, look at you, home so soon? Did you just have an awful time? This is New York City! I certainly didn't expect you back before dawn."

JOANNE, ANDREA, AND IVY

October 19, 2000
Ithaca, NY

Joanne takes Andrea's hand but she shakes it away. It's not that she doesn't feel they can hold hands here, per se, it feels safe enough, but she's not sure she can do it. Anywhere. Maybe ever again. Connect to another person right now, even *her* person. They were supposed to be leaving with a baby. Maybe her time on this planet being connected to anyone is over.

"She's keeping her," Andrea says, walking through the parking lot slightly ahead.

"We don't know that," says Joanne, her head down. She is trying to get the image out of her head of Bridget holding the baby tightly to her chest. The way she had looked up at them both so plaintively. It would be hard after seeing that, it's true.

"We can't take a child from someone who wants to keep her. It's wrong."

"She's a child herself. She doesn't know what's best yet," Joanne says. "When she was rational, she made a plan and she chose us."

They go to their car and Joanne gets in the driver's seat.

Andrea is sobbing. "Rational? It was before she had her baby."

Joanne places a hand over Andrea's shoulder and she shakes it off. "We can't take that girl's baby. Not if she wants her! This is all so messed up." She looks over, "I wish you were a man!"

Joanne stares at her, stunned.

Andrea starts laughing. "I so don't wish you were a man. I don't know why I said that. It just would have been easier. The kid stuff, I mean, you know? Logistically, it might have saved us." She reaches for Joanne's hand.

There.

Finally. Joanne looks over at her girlfriend. Her partner. Her wife. Her person. What if she is never the same now? That light in her eyes. It could be gone now. Never to return. "I love you," Joanne says softly. "This is going to happen for us." She is gripping the wheel but she doesn't turn the key.

Andrea shrugs. "Let's go to that café. Remember the one with the bluebirds? Where we had tea after we met her the first time."

Joanne nods and, as if remembering, she turns on the car and pulls out of the hospital parking lot toward the highway and the café. She remembers it, too. It had felt like a house that was about to fall into a creek and they'd had the most hopeful afternoon there after meeting Bridget for the first time.

They will order scones and tea and they will sit side by side on that little bench in the café and they will gather themselves up, together.

And they do. They go there and they sit down in that same spot looking out over the creek and the scones are warm, with oats and currants, and they add fresh butter because who cares now?, and they hold hands across the table and they put their new flip phone on the table, the phone they got so they could

talk to birth mothers at any time. And they do what they have
been doing for so long now. They wait.

And they wait and they wait and they finish up and wipe
away invisible crumbs and Joanne puts the phone in her pocket
and they go back to the Holiday Inn in town, which takes dogs,
but they didn't bring Pearl and Passion because they were supposed to be there with a baby. The baby would meet the dogs
at home, they'd thought. They will only worry about the baby.

They have diapers and a portable bassinet. They have no mes-
sages at the desk and they go upstairs and kick off their shoes
and snuggle up on the king-size bed and watch the gray sky turn
dark.

And the phone doesn't ring.

No one calls.

They wait and wait and none of the phones in the room ring
and dawn comes and they are both still awake, and then the gray
morning, thick with clouds and a cold autumn rain, a steel sky.
They rise, together, bend over their suitcases filled with bright
white onesies and glass bottles that clank together now.

They zip up. They close up. They button up and snap up.
They go downstairs and check out. And then they go home
together, alone.

IVY

2017
New York City

"My meeting got postponed," I say to Gram while looking hard at the knife I am using to spread obscene amounts of raspberry jam on my croissant. I see my eyes flash and glint in the silver. My head hurts. I haven't showered.

"Well, good you'll have the day today, then. Have you rescheduled?"

"I have," I say. Is she, like, going to pretend I'm meeting with a college counselor or something? Is she truly not going to ask me about this? It's so insane the way Gram is talking about this whole thing. Or not talking. But in a way, I guess, it's easier.

"Shall we phone your mother?"

"My mothers?"

"Yes, yes, your mothers."

"I texted earlier. They're alive and well. I'm good. I'm in touch with them just fine."

"Well then," Gram says. "Everyone settled okay?" She looks over to Claire and Patrick, who are also paying very close attention to their breakfast pastries.

They nod furiously.

"Well, I'm going down for a swim, then," says Gram. It is

something she is very proud of, her swimming. That she still swims. That she has swum, would swim, swims, will forever swim.

"Terrific, Gram," I say. I watch her pad off to her room, her robe flying behind her in a busy witch sort of way. I wonder if she will come out in her bathing suit and bathing cap for my friends the way she used to for my mothers.

She peeks out of her door and into the hallway. "Ivy, dear?" she says.

I look up. "Yes?"

"A moment?" she asks.

I get up and obediently follow her into her room.

"Darling." She closes the door. She holds her arms out to me. She is warm and she smells like roses. She puts her dry powdery hand on the side of my face. The duvet on her bed is all crumpled and lived in, not perfectly made as usual, and I notice Claire's book, *New York Foundlings*, is butterflied, facedown next to her pillow.

Gram's eyes are shot through with red. "Will you meet her today?" she asks.

"I think so," I say, grateful that finally she is asking me. That she cares. "I don't exactly know yet." I search her face but she doesn't offer me anything.

Gram holds me tight, to her heart. "I understand."

"No, you don't!" I laugh, but it turns into a little cry, too.

"I do, darling," she says. "Better than you know. I am not a monster." She takes in air, like she is sipping it, about to tell me something. "I . . ."

I wait.

She shakes her head, to herself really.

"I didn't think that," I say. "Anyway, I just want to see her, you know? Finally." I shrug. "I can't explain it."

"I imagine it will be wonderful," Gram says, patting my hair and kissing the tippy-top of my head.

I look at my grandmother, her eyes filling with tears. "I don't know," I say.

"If you think you want to see her, then you must!" She dabs her eyes with a balled-up handkerchief she's removed from her robe pocket. "Or you will regret it," she says. "Believe me. You will be filled with regret if you have the chance and you don't do it."

She takes her thumbs and rubs my cheekbones, hard. It feels like she's erasing me. "These cheekbones!" she says. "Like the Alps, I tell you."

Gram. "Thank you, Gram," I say, hugging her back.

"Of course," she says, straightening. "Now go on and let me get ready for my swim."

"Kooky Gram," I say when I get back to the table.

"I like her," Claire says. "I want to draw her."

I imagine Gram being drawn by my friend, just constantly looking at what she's doing, not really going with it, saying, *Oh, my, do you think I have those eyebrows, really, dear? I see.*

"She's got your orphan book in there," I say as I go and check the adoption registry site. Yesterday in the park when Patrick sent the note feels like three thousand years ago.

Claire looks over my shoulder and I don't know why but I shield the phone with my hand.

"Really?"

Suddenly this feels private to me. Maybe it just has been all along.

I look up from my phone. "Let me just see if there is anything after last night, okay?"

Maybe it's my serious tone but she turns back to her breakfast, dabbing jam onto another croissant.

The registry. Sure enough, two red dots. One, I am assuming, confirming my own response—well, Patrick's—and the other, well, perhaps it is from her. I click on.

Hi, Andrea. I am already doing my hours at PS 30 in Harlem. Taking classes still but doing this for credit three mornings a week. You probably don't know this school—let's just say not in your part of town, I don't think? It's amazing and I am lucky to do this work, to have these students and to be in the world this way. I am ready to meet Ivy when she is ready to meet me. This is my email if you or she or Joanne would like to communicate with me: Bridget2000@gmail.com. Not running anymore. I hope you all are thriving.

"Harlem," I say out loud, and for a moment I feel like I'm in one of those stories I read when I was little where these kids got clues from a librarian and then travel to all these places in their magic tree house. All they have to do is point to a place on a map.

Patrick stares out the huge window, sort of vacant like. I watch him and think of last night, Patrick, who was almost my *lover* but now is my best friend. I see how it flips around in all these good ways. I love him.

But now I am feeling anxious and just ready to go. And I suddenly realize maybe it's best to go it alone today. Actually, I am quite sure of it and I'm sure I've known it all along.

I'm about to say so when, as predicted, out trots Gram.

"Off to swim!" she says.

She looks like she has sprung out of the pages of one of Claire's vintage fashion photo books. Flowered bathing cap, blue one-piece that seems to be cutting off her circulation at the thighs, some kind of cork-wedged sandal that is also flowered, metallic, sequined terry robe, goggles swinging in hand, an Hermès towel hooked over her other arm. She is turned to the side and one leg is bent, photo-ready.

We are all speechless. We are staring. I watch Patrick slowly close his mouth.

"Amazing!" says Claire, standing. "You look a-mazing."

"Would you like to join, darling?" says Gram, shuffling toward the door. "Pool is just downstairs and, lucky for you, you know a very prominent member!"

"No suit!" Claire says, bringing her hands up, empty.

"Anyone else, then?"

"No, Gram," I say. "Have fun."

"Ta!" she says, and, truly, goes out, dressed this way, out into the rotten cabbagey-smelling hallway.

We don't say anything because really, what can we say?

I want to get going. My bones ache with wanting to leave.

"You know what?" I say to Claire and Patrick. "Let's separate and meet back in a few hours."

"What?" Patrick snaps to attention and he looks away from the view of the swath of blue sky.

"That's ridiculous," Claire says.

Patrick looks at Claire and takes a breath. "Do you need me?" he asks.

Claire rolls her eyes.

"I needed you both to get me this far," I say. It's true. I never would have gotten down here without them. Detour and all. "But I want to just go by myself, I really do."

"Okay," Patrick says.

Claire nods. She looks at Patrick. "We'll wait for you here," she says.

I imagine Gram coming back from her swim. I don't even know what that will look like and what seeing them here will mean for her.

"You should go out," I say. "Walk around, something, I don't know. It's New York City, kids! I don't think I'm going to be that long." I shrug. "I mean, I have no idea."

"You sure?" Claire asks again.

"I think I just want to gather and, like, do it on my own. I just do. You guys are so amazing to be here for me and do all this. I mean I have the best friends. Hashtag blessed!"

"Stop it," Patrick says.

"Okay, truly, then. Blessed for sure. Thanks for coming with me. I don't know what the day is going to be, so I just want to do it on my own."

Claire smacks her hands on her legs. "All right, then!" she says.

"Or stay around here, whatever," I say. I push back my seat and throw my napkin on my chair. "Draw my insane, mysterious, vintage grandmother," I say.

Patrick stands, too. "Are you sure?" He touches my elbow.

I nod. I smile. "I'm sure," I say. I push my chair out. "I'm going to shower in Gram's bathroom."

Patrick nods.

"What should we do today, Patrick?" Claire asks.

"There's not much around here," I say. "But you can walk to the Met. I remember walking to the Met for some reason."

"I could do that," Patrick says.

"Maybe we can find a great cover."

"What, you're going to put Rembrandt on the cover of *Crossroads*? Or a mummy?" I ask.

Claire ignores me. "How about," Claire says to Patrick, "we go for a run?"

Patrick shakes his head. "No," he says. "I will walk briskly with you to the Met, though."

Claire laughs.

"You guys can shower in the guest bathroom." I nod, not necessarily suggesting anyone needs a shower, but just letting them know it's a good option. "There are towels in there and everything."

They both nod and I pad off for my shower.

* * *

I go into Gram's room, which is a funny thing to do when she's not in it. It's all her stuff—blue glass bottles and lamps and reading glasses—and her rose smell and her bed is still unmade, as if she got up and left her imprint, an angel in snow.

Claire's book is gone now and then I see it on Gram's bureau, next to a dusty dried Japanese flower arrangement in a square black veneer vase.

I take the book. It's closed, but it opens easily to the page it had been open to clearly for some time.

On the left side of the page, there is a photo of a massive building, sort of off-white brick, the site of some kind of horror movie to be sure and on the right there is a photo of a baby. She's seated on a cushion, in an old-fashioned white nightgown. Her hair is black and shaggy as can be. You can tell someone tried to comb it to no avail. "Lulu," *Susquehanna Valley Home for Orphans,* it says in the caption. *February 1957.*

All babies do look the same to me, but there is something so familiar about her. Maybe it's the rouge on her cheeks, which looks strange in the black-and-white photo, that is so similar to the photo of Gram hanging above the stairs in my house. There's this mop of shaggy hair, but it's not just the hair and it's not just the strange photo coloration. It's the shape of the eyes, too, and just the way they look out at the camera. It also reminds me of one of the baby pictures I've seen of my mother. She doesn't have that hair, but the eyes are the same. And the little coin purse of her mouth, too.

I can't place this baby's face.

You will be filled with regret, Gram just said to me, and for a moment, I wonder if this baby is her. But then, cursing my math skills, I realize, that is impossible, of course it can't be Gram. It's from 1957.

Perhaps this was when Gram was in school, I think. I think of Claire, too. There are just so many reasons a person can look at a photograph. So many things to see.

I close the book and place it back on the bureau. I go into the bathroom and turn the shower on hot hot hot, the warm steam already rising when I step inside.

When I'm all showered, my night in Brooklyn, my night of almosts, scrubbed off my skin, I head back out to Patrick and Claire. I go to take Claire's book back to her and something stops me. I hold the book again and again it falls open to the picture. "Lulu." Is it that all babies from that time looked the same or is it that she looks like my mother?

It's something you can't see but it's there. For a moment I wonder if my mother is adopted. And she doesn't know it! But then I can't shake all the pictures of Gram and Grandpa Harry holding her in the hospital, Gram turbaned and eyelined and rouged but still wearing that been-through-a-war look. I don't think even Gram could stage that look.

When I go out to Patrick and Claire, they haven't moved much and they're working on their second pastries.

"We're going," Claire says when I come out, as if I care.

I so do not care. "This is yours," I say to her.

Patrick intercepts it and thumbs through it, also ending up

on the marked page. "These look just like the ones in your weird baby photo museum," Patrick says.

"What weird baby photo museum?"

"The one along the stairway in your house," he says. "Inescapable."

Claire is laughing.

"You, with the hanging crystals and burning incense are going to tell me my house is weird?" I say.

They both nod. "Eerie." Claire shakes her head. She cocks her head and looks at the photos again. "These are so sad. I never thought about them. I guess I just thought they were cool photos. And weird. But really they're mad sad."

I think of that girl in this horrible huge building. Was she all alone? Did people take care of her and kiss her and change her and love her? I can't help but wonder if I might have ended up in a place like this. It could have happened. A different set of butterflies; a different set of wings. I feel so sad for this baby. What happened to her?

"I wonder who she became," I say.

Claire nods. "I hope it was everything."

This catches my heart.

I can only know all the becames in my own story. I must find them. This is what I know.

I don't know why, but I go and place the book back on my grandmother's bureau, just where I found it. So she won't notice anything was missing at all.

IVY

2017
Uptown

Milton is back because it's daytime and so, when I get down-stairs, he salutes me and then when I ask he tells me there is a nice place to sit across from Gram's, by the river. I don't have a plan but it's this beautiful, breezy spring day. I sense every-thing thawing out, the heavy feel of winter disappearing from my bones.

I go to the bench and I do what I thought I might do soon but haven't done yet.

Which is take out the letter.

The one I haven't read yet.

I put it back in my jean jacket pocket and look out at the water, sparkling, sun catching water like knives turning in the light. I know reading this will change me, but I don't know how.

I take it out again and hope the change will be for good. I trace my fingertips over my mothers' names distorted by the bulk of the small item inside. But it is Bridget's handwriting, my first mom shaping the letters that makes the words that are my parents.

It's too much so I just tear it open, screw eighteen, and also? Screw letter openers. Inside: a feather. It's got downy fuzzy bits and then this sort of deep indigo blue in the silkier parts. It's bent a little on its long stem.

I twirl it in my fingers as I read the letter.

July 31, 2016

Dear You,

You. You are eighteen. Or maybe you're twenty-one. Or thirty-five. Maybe you're an old lady. What matters is you're reading this now. As I write it's about to be a new year. You must have so many questions. This letter doesn't have all the answers. But there are some things I would like you to know.

I want to tell you the story of you. I'll start by saying your birth father and I were in love, if you were wondering. Well, I loved him more, I see that now, but we loved each other and I want you to know that. He was a good guy, just a boy at the time. We had already broken up when I found out about you—you!—but he was there for me and he was there when you were born.

So were your mothers, as I'm sure they've told you. So was my mother. And my best friend. I hope you have a best friend like I had. She was there for me and she was a beautiful person. People grow apart. You probably know that by now, and we did. I left her behind, too, but I do really miss her.

You were born on a day I went for a walk in the woods. I did that a lot, but on the day you were born I found this beautiful nest that had fallen. One perfect blue robin's egg was inside. And next to the nest was a pile of feathers. Some bloody. And all these cracked blue eggs, too. I was so pregnant and hormonal and it upset me that I couldn't find the mother and that these eggs were all smashed. I found one of her long tail feathers. Well, I thought it was hers—but of course I know now the females don't have color. This could belong to the male that caused all the problems—but I didn't think of that then. I kept it while I was in labor with you. I kept thinking of the one blue egg. I kept thinking of you and the nest and me next to it trying to save you.

I've enclosed that feather. I kept it for all these years and I want you to have it so that you can have something to hold that has everything to do with how you came into this world.

I cannot lie to you now. I tried to keep you. I couldn't bear to be apart from you. Having you was the most important thing that I have ever done. It was amazing and awful and so painful and we had already been together for so many months! I had talked to you and sang to you and cried to you. And so when I met you I could not bear to leave you. Or place you with the parents I had worked so hard to choose for you.

I want you to know I took you home with me. I sort of ran away with you. And it was not because I was coerced or you were bad or cried too much or anything like this that I decided to go with my original adoption plan. You were perfect and beautiful and you were like a gift I didn't believe I deserved. Being with you made me realize that I could not be with you.

But I had to be with you to know that.

It's funny—I had no choice at all in my life and also I had all the choices. I could have placed you with any of the families I spoke to. People in finance. Rich New York City folks. Artists. A dancer. Some jerks in real estate in my town. You could be anyone now. It was like I was making you and I was also making you. That kind of choice was too much.

All the lives you could have led.

And then there was the choice of me.

Which didn't seem like a good option for you. I was sixteen. I wanted the best for you because I loved you—I love you—so much. I wanted to choose parents who were me but one thousand times better. Your moms were that. They are wonderful people who I know have helped make you into a wonderful woman.

I know now that adoption is always the story of someone breaking someone else's heart. But whose heart? It changes. I took you home and I broke your moms' hearts. I gave you back to them and my heart broke and broke. Did I break your heart, too? Or did I give you something bigger and better than I could have ever offered you?

I couldn't stick around to know.

I left my town after that. I went west. I did some bad stuff to just not be me. I went to Seattle. I bartended. I ended up in Wyoming and there I started learning a lot about nature, which I have always felt small in. In a good way. I started spending my life outside because every time I went inside I couldn't breathe. I felt like I had wings and they were flapping against some windowpane. I worked on a ranch. I worked for the Park Service. And eventually I became a guide—people would have me lead their kids up mountains. Rich kids.

But it was always kids. I didn't get along so well with grown-ups.

That first time I reached a summit? It was like how I felt when I had you. Only I got to do it for me.

I am leaving nature now. I have my reasons. One day I hope to tell you them.

Here's the rest of the story. When I called your moms and they came to get you? They came to our house. They were breathless for you. And I was not there when my mother handed you over. But what I heard was this: your silence. The moment they entered the house you stopped crying. It made me know you chose them, too.

Maybe it meant nothing, maybe it meant everything. I watched you go, out the door, into their car, silently.

I thought of all I would be now, and all that you would be.

I watched you drive away. If only, I thought, if only.

I have never known how to finish that sentence.

Until now. I am writing to tell you what I know now. The soul is every part of us. Our present, our past, our future. I saw my soul on those summits, at the horizon, in the branches of the trees. It's not just the now that we are living for. We are living for the past and because of it we are living for the future, too. Our dreams. That is also what is to come. All the things we might have been and who we might be. I thought I could control those things and I could not. I was sixteen and I let you go.

That is who we are. All the if onlys.

I can't get that song my friend's mother used to listen to all the time out of my head: You're sad and you're sorry but you're not ashamed, little green. Have a happy ending.

Did you? I hope I gave you a happy ending.

All of my love. And a feather. My feather.

Your first mom

When I'm done I look up at the river. It still flows. The sun is still shining. I'm still sitting on this bench. But it's all different. I can't say why or how but the whole world is different.

I draw the feather across my wrist. The slightest tickle. It makes me sad. I read the last part several more times. Am I living for the past or for the future? How do we ever know? In some ways it feels the same to me.

I look at the date and realize she wrote this to me only eight months ago. She was probably in this city by then. I look out at the river now and think of my moms waiting for me. How they waited for me sixteen years ago. I'm sad for Bridget, who does not, today, feel like my mother. But tomorrow she might feel more like my mother than anyone. If I go find her.

Is this a happy ending?

The wind whips my hair a little and I feel it knocking at my letter, like it wants to skip it along the sidewalk and then carry it into the air, high into a tree, where it will be tangled there in the bare branches. But I hold on tight; I fold it up into a tiny square and put it in my jacket pocket. I grip the feather securely, too. I brush it across my forehead, along the insides of my wrists. I think of the smashed eggs, the torn, bloody feathers.

I think of a nest. I think of one blue egg, cushioned inside, safe from harm.

The one that was saved.

THE GIRLS

October 25, 2000
New York State

Five days later, after leaving the hospital and the Holiday Inn that was no holiday at all, Andrea is pulling baguettes out of the oven when the flip phone on the kitchen counter rings. Andrea jumps at it—no one calls the cell. Only her mother and Joanne have the number. And Bridget.

She goes to it, more with curiosity than with anything else.

"Hello?" Bridget's wobbly voice. There is the sound of a baby crying in the background.

"Hello," Andrea says, breathing. She is scared to move. If she moves, she is certain the whole world will explode. She can't even wave down Joanne, who she can see outside in her canvas gardening gloves and those silly orange plastic clogs, bent over, pulling the tomato stakes down for winter.

"I have your baby," Bridget says.

"Bridget." Andrea pauses. "She's your baby."

"I don't know anymore," she says. "I don't know. But I think she is yours."

Andrea tries to catch her breath.

"Please," Bridget says. "Just come."

* * *

When they bring the baby home the following night, she is already six days old. They cannot think about the first five days of her life, and, least of all, this day, the sixth one. The day they took her away. It had been too much. The sadness of it was too much.

There were two ways of looking at it, really. Either today is the day everyone's heart broke or it is the day that they all chose each other.

And this is how Joanne and Andrea choose to see it. This is the day they all chose each other, a beginning of the mending of all the hearts. Bridget will be a part of their family. They will share everything. Andrea imagines baking bread each week and bringing warm loaves, along with Ivy, of course, they have kept her name, the perfect name, and a handful of Joanne's roses, for visits in town. Maybe they will show Bridget how to garden. Maybe Bridget can stay with them. Overnight. They will keep a guest room open for her, always, and they will finally build that terrace outside and cook big dinners. Maybe, this way, no one will be hurting. Ivy will know everything from day one. Well, day six.

Ivy sleeps in their bed tonight, even though it is cautioned against. Andrea knows she won't be sleeping; there is no way she will crush the baby. As she watches her sleep, her *daughter*, a word she can think but doesn't yet feel to be true, is curled up like a potato bug, that hand flung out of its swaddle in some sign of victory, that is what she chooses to believe. They chose each other. All of them. This is what she tells Joanne, on the other side of the baby, perched, a mirror image of Andrea, staring at this beautiful infant between them.

We are all in this together, they are thinking. Our family is big and bright and here we are on this wonderful planet together, all of us together, all of us a part of this beautiful world.

PS 30 is also called the Hernandez/Hughes School, in case anyone you know is looking for it. I look on my phone how to get
there but it's complicated and I decide to take another taxi.

I go back to Milton and he hails one down for me, slaps the
back of the trunk like it's some girl's bum, as we pull out of York
Avenue and circle back. I don't feel like talking, which is weird
for me in a taxi, like it's hard for me when I'm getting a haircut. I
always feel like I have to chat. To make everyone feel okay.

"Visiting?" the driver asks.

I nod and look out the window.

I don't know what I feel. I am nervous and sad and excited
and I know I should have let her know I was coming. For her and
also for me. I also know I will not turn back now.

"What are you doing up in Harlem?" the driver asks me.

"I'm looking for someone," I say.

He chuckles. "Okay, Detective," he tells me, and I let myself
smile. "East Harlem is full of someones, I'll tell you that."

The city changes. Doorman buildings and wide, empty
streets but for ladies walking teeny dogs by the river changes to
tons of people hanging out on the street, on stoops, in front of

stores. Lots of stands sell candy and some fruit, different kinds of Spanish food. Even the dogs are different: bigger, for one. Lots of pits, who get a bad rap because really they are the sweetest dogs around.

The taxi pulls up in front of the school, which is as big as a city block, just massive. I pay him, watch him drive away, look at a sign that says: *Education Opens the Door to WHO you can Be.*

I text Patrick and Claire. *Here,* I write.

Right away Patrick texts back, there he is, swoooop, dimpled chin, some zits around the hairline. Boy smile. *You okay?*

Nothing yet, I text.

Did you meet her?

Nope, I say. *Heading in now.*

Lemme know, B. Love you.

Me 2, I write.

I love that there were no emojis to pass between us. A feat, I think.

I gather myself up and go to the door, but it's locked.

Phone buzzes.

Claire writes, *Hey! Good luck. P and I are hanging and we miss you. Who knew the Met was so hard to find. We're rambling!*

Fun! I write and I love thinking of them wandering around together.

Be strong! she writes.

I smile. *OK.*

And then I can't stop myself: smiley face, kiss, prayer hands, heart, city, city, city, heart.

Love you, she texts back. She attaches a picture, a photo of the drawing she made of me. *Ivy, Searching. Just so you know*, a new text comes in. *We have our Crossroads cover. Here it was, all along.*

And then: muscle, hands praying, kiss

The next door is locked—and by locked I mean, does not budge—and then the next and the next but finally I find a side entrance that's open. A security guard stops me.

"Yes?" he asks.

"I'm looking for someone," I say.

He chuckles, a deep, comforting laugh. "Honey, this is a school, for little kids. You can't just walk in here and look for someone."

"Can I go to the office, then?"

"You may," he says, and he guides me through a bunch of hallways—really old-feeling ones—and to an administrative office. He sort of pushes me inside and walks away, back to his post I guess.

I look at the three people at the three different metal desks. All women. I try to decide who the nicest one will be and I settle on the one I believe to be the oldest, who also has cropped hair and massive earrings, shaped like suns. She has on red glasses and she peers over them at me when I go to her desk.

"Yes?" she says.

I take a deep breath. "Okay," I say. "Here is the story," I begin.

I tell her about my birth mother. And my mothers. And that she's here and I should have told her but I didn't. And that I just want to see her.

"I came all this way," I say. My hands are in my jacket pockets and I'm rocking back and forth on my toes. "I just want to see her. And then I'll go."

"I'm Nadia," the woman says. She takes off her glasses with one hand and then she holds out the other hand to shake mine.

"Ivy," I say. Her hands are strong and comforting.

She stands up and walks slowly to the front of her desk, which is piled high with papers. All kinds of papers and all kinds of piles. I think of Mo's description of her own messy desk: it means I'm in *process*, Mo says. Mo.

"Well, she is here, I will tell you that," says Nadia, leaning on her desk. "She's a student teacher."

"I see," I say.

"I don't know what the policy on this even is, but I do see your urgency. I have adoption in my family, too," she says. "But that's a different story." She crosses her arms.

"Okay," I say. I have no idea what Nadia is about to say to me.

"I'll just say that she is on the third floor. She teaches science. To fifth graders."

I am listening but my ears feel blocked.

She is waiting for me to move, I can tell, but I just stand there. I can't move.

"Okay, then," Nadia says, and then she walks toward the door and I, relieved, follow her out, and to the stairs, but I don't have any idea where we are going. There is this insane ringing in my ears. It's like I'm on a plane and I can't adjust to the pressure no matter how much I chew the gum Mom has handed me for that moment when we rise into the sky.

We pass all kinds of classrooms and through the little windows at the tops of the doors I can see kids are singing with all their hearts and watching movies and painting crowns and teachers are writing on boards and leaning on their desks and pointing to maps and everyone seems kind of happy. Well, they all seem like they belong. The walls are this hideous pale yellow, and pretty dirty, but there are also whiteboards with maps and letters and kids' drawings and directions and all kinds of lovely stuff.

Then Nadia stops. She takes my elbow and leads me to the door. And then she stands back. And then, and then and then. I look inside.

The first thing I see is all the children. Maybe twenty of them, each holding his or her face up to a rolled-up tube of paper. They look at her through their paper rolls as if they are looking through telescopes. She is behind a desk holding her own cylinder, and she says, "Now take your rolls and imagine they are bird bones. Bird bones are hollow, just like this." She places a finger inside the tube.

I stand there, watching her. I don't think about Nadia, standing next to me because there she is. She has: white skin, like mine, super white. And dark hair, which is shiny, like mine is. Hers is cut short, with a streak of blond at the front. She has eyes that are widely set apart, like mine, and hers are that same gray-blue I have been looking at in the mirror for all these years. She is wearing a long feather earring in one ear and the other ear is bare. And her nose. I imagine tracing it with my finger, but instead, without meaning to, I feel myself touch my finger to my own nose.

On her desk there is a nest and also a rock shaped like an egg, that same white stone color I have. There is a feather. They are all together here.

Her hands hold the roll of paper and she looks at the class through it. Her hands.

The kids all laugh and look back at her.

And she laughs, too.

Her laugh. My laugh.

"Now," she says. "Let's take three of these bones and put them on the table and let's set a plate on them. How strong are a bird's bones? How many coins can these hollow bones hold?" She stands up. "Let's find out!"

She comes out from behind her desk. And then I see it. Her belly! She has an enormous stomach and she rubs it as she waddles to the front of the classroom. She is going to have another baby.

I finally find her just as she is about to be someone else's mother.

I am leaving nature now, she wrote. *I have my reasons.*

And now I see them. I see everything. *I am writing to tell you what I know now. The soul is every part of us. Our present, our past, our future. I saw my soul on those summits, at the horizon, in the branches of the trees.*

In there could be the third girl. I could have a sister.

She sets out huge piles of bright copper pennies. The children have all gone to their tables with their paper plates, building birds. "Estimate how many pennies you think this bird can hold," she says. I see her high forehead—like mine—crinkle up a bit as she watches the children place the plates on the birds' bones. *It's not just the now that we are living for. We are living for the past and because of it. We are living for the future, too. Our dreams.*

"How many do you think?" she asks.

That is also what is to come. All the things we might have been and who we might be.

The children add one coin at a time. Behind her the board says *Life Sciences*. In her handwriting. I know her grown-up handwriting now.

I watch, too, thunderstruck. One of the pretend birds goes down and the kid says, "Damn," and stomps his foot.

"Jerome, how many coins did it take? It's a lot! Hollow bones are still strong bones."

She walks around the room, touching the corners of tables. I watch her check her watch. "Just a few more minutes, guys!" she says. "Let's finish up!"

I was sixteen, she wrote, *and I let you go.*

That is who we are. So many if onlys.

Lost or found. I think, suddenly, of that "Lulu" in the book. Was she ever found? Unwanted or special, chosen. It's impossible to say. In that room is my first mother. And a sibling, too. That nest on the desk. The rock like an egg. All the feathers. All the butterfly wings. Here we are, all of us. Downed birds. And here we are, still, all of us flying.

The students are putting away their materials and packing up for the day. They concentrate hard as they organize their coins and pretend bones; they smile each time they pass her and she smiles back. Above my head a bell rings, madly, and the students begin to file out, in clumps, alone; they are moving on. And then they are gone. The door is closed again.

I watch as she stands to face the board—*Life Sciences*—her arms crossed. Then she unfolds, picks up an eraser.

And then I do something that I don't entirely expect. I make a choice. I choose. I nod at Nadia and she nods back. I turn the handle and then, very softly, I step quietly inside.

ACKNOWLEDGMENTS

Thank you to Jen Klonsky, an editorial delight, who helped me wrestle this out of the ether and into a form. Thanks to the wonderful team at Harper Teen and to Jenn Joel, my agent, who really cheered this project on. Big thanks to Joanna Hershon, my first reader, and to Hyatt Bass, Lola Calotychos, Meg Wolitzer, and Nina Revoyr for their ever-helpful early reads. Thank you to Pedro who has been living with this material for a long time. Adoption is big and hard and complicated for everyone involved, and I want to thank the people who helped and supported my family as we went through the long process. Jovi and Andrew I thank here and everywhere.